A
HIGHLAND
Home

A CONTEMPORARY HIGHLAND ROMANCE
BOOK TWO

CALI MACKAY

A Highland Home
by Cali MacKay
Copyright © 2012 by Cali MacKay
Published by Cali MacKay
http://calimackay.com

Printed in the United States of America
First Printing, 2012, first edition
ISBN: 978-1-940041-09-4

Contents

For Joe, Maeve and Amelia.

CHAPTER
One

THE PUNGENT AND salty sea air filled Rowan's lungs as the wind from the open window whipped through her hair, tugging her red locks loose. She took in the craggy cliffs and heather, the sparse beauty and desolation. It was at once so new and yet it felt incredibly familiar, even if the Scottish highlands were nothing like the mountains of Vermont.

More importantly, this felt like home. It was a new start to a new life—and that left her feeling giddy, like champagne bubbles had tickled her nose.

"We're nearly there now. I'm sure ye'll be wanting to get settled in. Ye must be exhausted after such a long trip." Angus's smile lit his blue eyes from within, his dark tumbled curls and rough stubble making him look ruggedly handsome and far too charming.

He was the son of her mother's best friend, and kind enough to collect her at the airport in Glasgow. Having studied veterinary medicine at Cambridge, his clipped lilt was mild and easy enough to understand, though her heart still raced to hear its melody.

"I think I'll end up sleeping for a week." She gave him a warm smile, her excitement refusing to be contained despite feeling jetlagged and exhausted. Now in her mid-twenties, she'd done a fair amount of traveling, but this was where she hoped to put down roots and finally get the answers she'd been searching for all her life. "I can't thank you enough, Angus—for everything."

Once she'd decided to make the move, Angus had been an amazing help. He'd even seen to updating the cottage that had been her grandfather's and then her mother's, both of them now gone, leaving her without any family. It was just a small home, she'd been told, sitting on the edge of a cliff to overlook the raging sea.

It couldn't sound any more perfect.

Angus threw her a sideways glance, before turning his attention back on the road. "There wasn't too much that needed doing, since the place has had tenants living there on and off. Still, it's probably a far cry from what ye're used to, aye?"

She took a look at the rugged landscape. Massive rocks seemed to jut out of the ground with no rhyme nor reason, and though it was a stark beauty, it was a beauty nonetheless. The amazing views would give her ample material to work with, and as an artist, it didn't matter that the closest city was hours away.

"I'm happy for the change and have been looking forward to this for a long time. I swear, I've never seen anything more breathtaking."

"Not many locals stay anymore, though we certainly get overrun with tourists due to the cliffs and the circle of stones. The town is picturesque too. Still, the last generation or two have left for the city as soon as they're able."

Like her mom. She'd left as soon as she could, the ink barely dry on her nursing degree when she headed for the States, never to return to her childhood home.

He pointed to a large home. "That there's your closest neighbor. Conall Stewart. Went to school with him. He can be a right bastard, but keeps to himself mostly. So if you're looking for a bit of company, you'll still be stuck calling me." He gave her a wink that made her laugh.

She looked at him with one brow perked in disbelief. "You make it sound like you're the only two people on the Firth."

"We are, unless you're looking for someone more grey and hunched over like. If that's the case, then old MacDougall might suit you fine." His sly smile had her laughing. "You think I'm teasing, but it's the truth. You'll find out soon enough. Unless, of course, you prefer the excitement of a brief affair—plenty of visitors to choose from, if that's yer preference."

She threw him a mischievous glance. "So my choices for entertainment are you, my cranky neighbor or a fling?"

"Aye, and don't forget the old crabbit MacDougall." When she caught his gaze with a stern look, he gave her a wink and a laugh. "Actually, there are a handful more people our age. My good friend, Iain, and his fiancé, Cat, aren't far from here. She's also American, by the way."

"Well, I'm glad I have more options than just crabbit MacDougall. But you can't tell me you're actually single." If he were in the States, she knew the women would be fighting for him hand over fist. Nice, smart, good-looking, successful and straight. It was a rare combination in her book.

He shrugged and threw a smile her way. "Had a lass when I lived in the city, but it ended when I decided to come back home and start my veterinary practice. It wasn't serious though, and she was off to London before I'd even finished packing my bags. What about yerself? Surely ye've left hoards of heart-broken lads pining after ye."

"Nope. No one left behind with a broken heart. I haven't stayed in one place long enough to really bother, and relationships always seem far too complicated." She wouldn't mention how she'd given her heart to Stephen and even agreed to marry him, only to find him screwing her roommate when her flight landed early. "I'm hoping to stay put this time around."

"Well, it makes me a happy man to hear ye'll be settling down in our wee little village." He gave her another sideways glance and a smile. "And since ye're choices are old crabbit McDonald, cantankerous Conall, and lovable old me, I'm liking my odds."

She burst out laughing. "You know, you really are incorrigible."

"Well, I do try, my dear." Another dashing smile.

Pity she'd sworn off men for anything other than the rare casual involvement—and there was something about Angus that made her think he did *not* do casual. It'd be one thing if they were in a big city, but it would be impossible to avoid him in a town this small, and frankly, she liked him way too much to let things get awkward between them.

He pulled her from her thoughts. "Rowan… I'm really sorry about yer mother. My Ma's still heartbroken over it. They were inseparable growing up."

Though it had been a year since her mother had passed, it was still hard to deal with. But being in the village where she grew up would be one more way to remember her. More importantly, she might finally get the answers to the questions she'd been asking her entire life—answers her mother refused to give her, even on her deathbed.

She tried to stay positive, not wanting to spoil things with sadness. "I'm hoping I might get the chance to speak to your mom about their adventures growing up. I'm sure they got into all sorts of trouble."

"I guarantee it." Angus turned the car down a gravel drive and put the car in park. "Here ye are."

The white-washed cottage was just as she'd imagined it. Diamond paned windows sat nestled in thick stone walls, the thatch most likely replaced at some point with slate. Wild pink roses clung to the walls, making it picture perfect, and off in the distance Rowan could see the ocean, the sun dipping towards the horizon.

She grabbed his arm and all but jumped for joy. "It's gorgeous, Angus. I can't believe I'm finally here."

"There's not much to the place, but the view can't be beat, and the stone circle is just over the hill there. Come, I'll show ye around. Door's open if ye want to head in. I'll be right behind ye with yer bags."

Rowan grabbed her carry-on and stepped into a blustery wind coming off the ocean, excitement and anticipation bubbling within like the swirling waters that crashed against the craggy cliffs. The stone path led to a red front door, bold and inviting. With a hand on the brass handle, she let herself in and stepped into the living area.

It was cozy and sweet. On one side, a long red sofa and chair sat by a small iron stove and TV, whereas the other side served as a dining room with a small table and chairs. Rowan moved beyond the living room to find a decent-sized kitchen, and a small bath. A small bedroom was being used as an office and would serve well as her studio. She then took the narrow stairs up to a large bedroom which occupied the entire floor.

Likely once an attic, the longest walls were short, before moving up into a sloped roofline. It could have felt claustrophobic, but the room was large and the ceiling height at its peak was generous, with several skylights aiding the airy feel. Two large windows on the opposite walls let the light pour in through the lace curtains, mottling the bedspread in shadows, while a cheery yellow danced on the walls.

"What do ye think? Will it do?"

Rowan turned to find Angus standing behind her, and had to resist the urge to hug him. After months of emailing him, months of him making sure everything was ready for her arrival, she couldn't thank him enough. "It's perfect."

"Glad to hear it. I stocked the kitchen with some basics, but ye might want to get to the grocer's before long. The keys to the car—a manual transmission, by the way—are hanging in the kitchen by the back door. But if ye're planning on staying, ye'll likely want to get yerself a more reliable vehicle."

"I'm definitely staying." Going back home was not an option—and definitely not until she got the answers she was looking for.

"Ye say that now, and it's a good thing we're heading into warmer weather, but wait until we're fully into winter nine months from now. I'll find ye on the first plane to Ibiza looking for a bit of sun and a handsome Spaniard." Another charming smile had her taking a deep breath to keep her pulse steady.

"I grew up in New England—cold winters don't scare me, my dear. And it'll take more than that to make me leave if I don't want to go. I'm stubborn—or so I've been told."

"Aye, well, that'd be the Scottish in ye." He wandered back towards the kitchen. "I left yer bags in the sitting room, and the boxes ye sent ahead of time are in the back entry just there. Ye've got my number should ye need it, but I'll warn ye now, coverage with a mobile can be spotty at times."

"Again, I can't thank you enough, Angus."

"I'll go so ye can rest and get yer bearings, but will swing by tomorrow to see how ye're fairing."

She walked him to the door, and saw him out with a final word of thanks before turning back to her new home.

And for once she felt like she belonged.

Rowan woke up in a strange bed, feeling lost as her mind tried to work through the grogginess and she tried to get her bearings. The sun filtered through the lace curtains as a slow smile spread across her face. Jetlagged, she still felt a bit off, but a not-so-hot shower worked wonders to wake her up and clear her head. Wrapped in a robe, she grabbed a bite to eat, and with a coffee in hand, felt all the more human for it.

After digging through her suitcases for jeans and a comfy sweater, she grabbed her camera, threw on her pea coat and boots, and headed for the door, ready to start her new life.

The fog clung to the heather in waves, as the sun broke through the clouds in streaks of brilliance. There was an ethereal quality to the light, the way it shone golden bright against the darkness surrounding it. With camera in hand, she adjusted her aperture and focus, and snapped one image after the other, the peace and energy of the place vibrating through her. As the light shifted, so did her focus, catching the ever-changing images before her.

Distracted by the photos she was taking, she heard the commotion heading her way before she saw it. Finishing her shot, she looked down to find a wiggling ball of wiry fur, the dog's tail whipping around with excitement.

"Where did you come from?" Rowan slung her camera over her shoulder and then crouched down to pet the pup. It was a bizarre mix of some sort of collie, with... greyhound? And maybe a bit of Jack Russell thrown in for good measure? Not terribly tall but with long spindly legs. Hyper little thing for sure, and cute as a button with a raccoon mask surrounding her eyes. No collar, but in good enough shape to not be a stray. "Did you escape? Or are you lost?"

And then she heard a voice being carried on the wind. *"Piper!"*

She had to laugh. "I take it that's you, right? Sounds like you might be in a bit of trouble."

A figure came up over the hill, the fog clinging to the ground by his feet. The dog paid him no attention, even if there was no doubt in Rowan's mind that he was the owner—and looking none too happy about it. She held onto the pup to prevent her from escaping.

"Is she yours?"

"Aye. Thanks for grabbing her." The man leaned forward and slipped the dog's collar over her head, adjusting it so it wouldn't slip free again. He then stood, and turned to go.

"I think we might be neighbors." This had to be the neighbor Angus had mentioned. Conall was it? A curious sort. Rough exterior with tumbled dark blonde hair, and scruffy stubble. Intelligent eyes in an unusual amber color.

With a sigh, he spun back to face her. "Are ye in the Campbell's cottage then?"

"I am. Just got here yesterday."

"Well, ye best be careful walking in the fog. Liable to fall into the sea." He looked at her camera and then back to her face, impatience in his stance. "Ye best head back. Leave yer photos for another day."

She should probably let him go, but if they were neighbors, then she'd like to know his name, at the very least. She stuck out her hand. "I'm Rowan. Rowan Campbell."

He sighed, and shook her hand, the feel of it strong and just a bit rough. "Conall Stewart—and Piper."

"I thought so." When his eyes narrowed in question, she added, "Angus Macleod mentioned you'd be my closest neighbor. He's a family friend."

"Hmph. I'm sure he is. Keep away from the cliffs and ye'll be fine." And with that, he turned and made his escape.

Rowan watched her neighbor and his dog walk away, the fog wrapping around them like a lover's embrace. Unable to resist, she snapped a picture, man and dog fading into the mists.

Angus warned her that her neighbor was a bit of a loner, but experiencing it firsthand brought it home for her. Cute dog, though—not that Conall wasn't something to look at. With loose curls the color of dark honey, gold eyes and a scruffy five o'clock shadow, it was all she could do to not smile at the mere thought of him. Between Conall and Angus, she was starting to think there must be something in the water.

Good thing she didn't have time for that sort of distraction. She'd come to Scotland with a set plan and goals, and she'd be damned if she was going to let a couple of men distract her, no matter how good-looking.

Getting back to work, she wandered for several more hours, taking photos of anything and everything, playing around with the settings on her camera for different effects. When she finally headed home, it was with her heart full and her spirit at peace. The fresh crisp air and the amazing views had energized and renewed her, reinforcing that this was a new start and a new life. And with luck, she'd soon have answers to the questions that had plagued her throughout her lifetime.

A smile sprung to her lips when she saw she had company. She wandered over to where Angus was leaning against his car. "You should've let yourself in. I hope you weren't waiting too long."

"Ye can make it up to me with a cup of tea." Angus tilted his head towards her camera and followed her into the house. "Were ye able to get any photos? The fog's been coming in waves all morning. If ye timed it just right, I'd think there might be some interesting shots."

Settling in the kitchen, she flicked her camera on and handed it to him so he could page through the shots she took. "Every now and then the light was amazing. I'm really looking forward to exploring the area further. Maybe drive up the coast."

"North of here is really beautiful. I'd be happy to take ye one of these days."

"I'd love to, but I feel guilty hogging all your time, especially when you've been such an amazing help. You'll be sick of me by the time summer rolls around." She filled the kettle at the sink, but when she turned to the stove, she quickly realized she wasn't sure how to use it. "I swear, I'm not normally useless in the kitchen, but right about now even boiling water is looking a bit tricky."

Angus laughed and got to his feet. He lifted the hinged cover on one of the top burners, set the kettle down, and turned the dial. "It's an Aga. I got it warmed up and going for ye the other day, so ye should be set since it'll keep itself running. It'll do a decent job of heating the house too, though ye've got the fire in the living room if need be."

He pulled open a cupboard and grabbed a couple of mugs, no doubt sparing her from going on a wild goose-chase through the kitchen. There was a powerful grace to his movements, and tall as he was, he seemed to fill the small kitchen. He brushed past her and sat back down at the table, picking up her camera once more and flicking through the images.

"The photos—they're *really* good." He ran a hand over his chin. "I don't know how ye do it, for I swear each time I drag out my camera, the photos ne'er look like this."

She knew exactly what he meant. It was one of the reasons she got into photography—too many mediocre pictures when she knew they could be amazing. "A bit has to do with the camera you're using, but it's often just a matter of taking it off the automatic setting and experimenting."

"And ye'll sell these?"

"Yep." She smiled, thinking of the mish-mash of ways she managed to keep an income coming in. There were several regular clients who used her for their graphics work, and made up for the bulk of her cash flow, though her collages, photos and paintings brought in a pretty penny when they sold, even if that income was less regular.

She continued. "I'll likely incorporate them into another piece, either digitally or within a painted composition. I'd be happy to give you a few pointers for taking pictures. It's the least I can do after all your help."

"Aye, I'd like that." Angus picked up the camera again and paged through the pictures, while Rowan poured the boiling water into a metal teapot with several bags of tea. When she returned to the table, he turned the camera to her, a man and a dog walking away in the fog. "Is that Conall?"

"Yeah, his dog got loose." She shook her head, a smile springing to her lips. "You were so right about him keeping to himself. He couldn't get away from me fast enough."

"Don't let him bother ye. He's ne'er been a great one for conversation." Angus pursed his lips, a shadow clouding his eyes. "Tea should be ready if you'd like to pour it. I'll grab the biscuits."

Rowan grabbed the mugs he'd put out and poured the tea, the fragrant steam hitting her in the face and warming her. She was still chilled from her walk, the weather brisk this early in the spring. "Milk and sugar?"

"Aye, love. How else would ye have it?"

She looked over her shoulder and smiled at him as he reached around her to the cabinet above and pulled down a package of cookies—or biscuits, if she wanted to be correct for the part of the world she was in. Their bodies brushed as they maneuvered in the small kitchen, and he plated the chocolate covered oat treats.

Settling in at the table, Rowan wrapped her hands around the hot mug to warm them and took a sip, the hot brew heating her from the inside out and making her feel whole again. Raised by a Scottish mother, she was a regular tea drinker, and since her last cup had been State-side, she was going through withdrawal. She liked coffee and it was usually what she had first thing in the morning, but from there, she usually lived on a steady stream of tea, especially when she was working.

Angus grabbed two biscuits, and with the chocolate sides sandwiched together, dunked them in his tea and ate them. "How'd ye spend the night? I hope ye managed to keep warm. Be sure to make use of the fire."

"It was quite comfortable. The blankets were enough, luckily." It was sweet of him to ask. "So, tell me more about Conall Stewart. I want to be prepared for the next time I see him."

He glanced at her over his tea with a tilt of his head. "There isn't much to know. Like I said, he's a bit of a loner. Does well enough for himself if his home and car are anything to go by. Why? Are ye interested? He's single, as far as I know."

"Nope. Not interested in the very least. Like I said, I don't do relationships. Not worth the headache, I'm afraid." She grabbed a biscuit and gave it a dunk, the chocolate quickly melting onto her fingertips. She licked them off out of habit, and saw his eyebrows inadvertently twitch up in response. Doing her best to not blush, she finished her train of thought. "I just like knowing who's around me. Sometimes neighbors can be... difficult."

"Aye, they can be." His brow furrowed in question. "But I still can't believe ye're so steadfast about relationships. Why's that, love? Ye're young, smart and pretty—I'd think ye'd have plenty of offers to choose from."

She didn't want to have to rehash the last few years of her life, and certainly didn't need his pity or to be reminded of how stupid she'd been. It still stunned her that she hadn't known Stephen was cheating, hadn't seen past his fun and charming façade. Nor had she figured out that it was with her good friend. She considered herself a pretty smart girl—or at the very least, not completely clueless. So then, how could she have been so blind? It left her angry with herself for not seeing what was right in front of her face. "Guess I just haven't found the right guy."

"I can understand that. Sometimes it's hard to find another ye might want to share yer life with."

Desperately trying to avoid any more relationship talk, she turned the conversation back to Angus. "So what's up between you and Conall? You don't seem to be the best of friends, if you don't mind me saying."

He shrugged and looked down at his tea, clearly avoiding her gaze. "I grew up with him, but there was a bit of history between our families— yours too, sorry to say."

"Oh. I hadn't realized." Must have been why she got a cold reception from Conall. "So what's that about then?"

Angus shrugged again, his gaze landing squarely on his cup of tea and refusing to stray. "Wouldn't really know any of the details, I'm afraid. Happened when I was just a bairn."

He was acting all sorts of funky, and it now had her wondering. "How old are you, Angus?"

"About yer age."

Rowan's mind raced. It'd be right around the time her mom left Dunmuir. Did the bit of bad blood between the families somehow relate to the clues she was looking for? She suspected Angus knew a hell of a lot more than he was letting on, and though he might help her if she opened up to him, she wasn't sure she was ready to go down that road.

The problem was she didn't have any idea who her father was. Her mother refused to talk about him—not a name, no hint as to what he was like, no reference to their time together. She had hoped her mom would finally tell her when she knew she had little time left, yet she'd still refused Rowan's requests. Even after she'd passed, there were no letters, no secret journal, no name. She did have a few clues, but they just weren't enough.

"Are ye all right?" Angus pulled her from her thoughts, his brow furrowed, his gaze locked on hers.

A smile sprung to her lips to keep Angus from asking any questions. "Sorry. Just got distracted."

He must have thought she was still dwelling on Conall. "Don't let Conall get to ye. He's always been a dour sort, and not worth the trouble. Smart—and I'll even give him handsome enough—but he's got a puss on him like he's drank sour milk."

Rowan burst out laughing, and the tension she'd felt only moments earlier, melted away. "Well, I'm glad to hear I'm not the only who has that effect on him."

He leaned forward with his elbows on the table, his blue eyes locked on hers. "Being a stranger to these parts, it'll take people awhile to warm up to ye. But don't take it personally, aye? They're just set in their ways, and not used to a whole lot of change."

It felt like he was preparing her for something, even if she didn't know what. "What aren't you telling me, Angus?"

With a shrug, he sat back and played with his mug. "There's ne'er much to tell in places like this, lass. Nothing out of the ordinary, aye? But the town's an old one, and is settled in its ways. I just want ye to give it a bit of time, is all."

"I don't scare easily, Angus." She managed a smile, determination in her gaze. Maybe he did know more than he was letting on.

"Happy to hear it." His smile widened and his eyes sparkled with mischief. "I need to see a client just north of here. Don't suppose ye'd like to join me? I won't be long, and would be happy to show ye around the place afterwards. Maybe take ye out for a bite."

"Only if you let me buy. I owe you big time for all you've done." It would be the perfect way to check out the area, since she was a bit iffy about driving herself. Not only was she not familiar with the area, but the car in the garage was a stick shift, and she didn't trust herself to not screw up the whole driving-on-the-opposite-side-of-the-road thing.

"Bring yer camera, aye? There are some gorgeous views where we'll be heading, and the fog may even clear up for ye."

The excitement of a new life and adventure bubbled inside her. Soon… she'd find the answers she was looking for. She'd find her father.

CHAPTER
Two

A NGUS CONCLUDED HIS examination, pulled off his gloves and tossed them into his bucket. "Tonight or tomorrow, I'm guessing."

He ran his hand over the mare's abdomen, swollen with the bairn within. The skin was taut like a drum, the muscles beneath like stone. The contractions had yet to start, but he suspected it wouldn't be long.

"She'll manage it just fine, I'm sure, but I've got yer number should I need it." Robbie McNally pulled an apple from his pocket with a weathered hand and fed it to Craggy, his favorite mare. He then tilted his head towards Rowan with a sly grin, as she wandered by the fence off in the distance, camera already out. "Who's the lass, Angus? Ne'er seen ye bring anyone around before. She's a pretty thing with all that red hair. Always been partial to it myself. But be fair warned—they tend to be the fiery sort. Independent too."

Angus ignored Robbie's laugh and jesting. "That's Rowan, a family friend. Just moved here from Vermont."

"Aye? Vermont?" Robbie's eyes narrowed with thought, before going wide. He then cocked his head back to look at her again. "Ye're not telling me she's Iona's girl, are ye?"

"She is." Angus felt his back go up. "And I'm telling ye now, whatever happened with her ma is in the past, and she's got nothing to do with it. She knows nothing of it, aye?"

"She'll find out soon enough once word spreads. Ye best keep yer distance, lad. Ye don't want that sort of trouble." Robbie shook his head and ran a hand over his bristled chin.

Angus leaned in, annoyed. "Whatever happened decades ago with her ma has nothing to do with her. Ye hear me? She'll be shown the highland hospitality we're known for. You make sure of it, and be sure to let the others know too, or they'll be dealing with me."

Robbie put his hand up. "Calm yourself, lad. I'm not going to run her out of town. But ye may want to warn her, aye? The Stewarts won't be happy about it and neither will anyone else in town, once they find out who she is. Things like that don't tend to die off easily."

"People need to let it rest. These days, no one would give any of it a second thought." He grabbed his bucket and medical kit, his movements tense. "Let the others know—I'll not tolerate any nonsense."

"I'll pass it on, lad. Just don't go falling for her, aye?"

Angus spun on him, every muscle knotted tight. "And why's that, Robbie?"

Robbie put up both hands and shook his head. "Forget I said anything. I'll call ye if there's any trouble with Craggy. If not, ye'll hear from me once the wee one's born."

"Aye. I'll see ye then."

Angus headed back to his Rover and tossed his things in the back, his shoulders still tight. His mother had warned him that Rowan wouldn't get a warm reception, but he hadn't quite believed her. It had been so long ago, and even if there was a lot more to the story, children were often born out of wedlock, and other than a bit of gossip, no one gave a rat's arse.

They'd eventually warm up to her once they got to know her—of that he had no doubt—and until then, he'd do his best to protect her from the truth. The last thing he wanted was for her to not feel welcome when she'd just arrived.

Rowan was already wandering over. "Did ye get any good pictures?"

The smile on her face melted away some of his anger—but not all. People would see past what happened with her mother, and would see Rowan for who she was. They just better do it quick, because he'd not have her feeling uncomfortable in a place that should feel like home.

Her brow furrowed as she laid a gentle hand on his arm. "Is everything all right?"

Surprised she'd notice, he forced himself to let it all go, pushing a smile onto his face. "Just getting hungry is all. Would ye like to get a bite?"

She smiled at him, her eyes dancing in the sunlight over a sea of freckles. "Only if you let me buy. I still owe you, yeah?"

"Och, well, if ye're buying then we might as well have a pint with our meal, too." He gave her a wink, happy to see her smiling.

"Well, you've certainly earned it."

Settled in a corner of the local pub, Angus set a few pints in front of them and slid into the booth across from Rowan. They'd made it there just in time. Soon after arriving, a bus of tourists pulled up and unloaded. The small pub was now bustling, barely a seat to be had.

He handed her a menu, not bothering to take one for himself. He'd been coming here for as long as he could remember, and other than the specials written on the chalkboard, the changes were kept to a minimum. "Their burgers are good. And ye can't go wrong with the fish and chips. They use fresh–caught from the local fishermen right here at the harbor."

"Sounds perfect." She closed her menu and gave him a smile as she looked around the place, taking it all in. "Is it always this busy?"

"That friend I mentioned and his fiancé? They recently found a diamond and emerald necklace of huge historical importance. It's tucked away someplace safe until they can figure out where they'll be putting it on display, but it put our little town on the map. The tourism has picked up as a result, despite the weather still being cold. I suspect the number of tourists will only increase as we head further into spring. Ye could sell yer photos to them, if ye wanted. Make yerself a good chunk of change, I'd imagine."

Her eyes sparkled, as if lit from within, the green of them like a stormy sea. "It's a thought. I've always wanted to open a small gallery and studio—not just for my own work, but to help other artists. Maybe teach a few classes. Might be worth looking into once I get settled. I hadn't realized Dunmuir had so many visitors."

By the gods, all those months of emailing back and forth had gotten to him. And to now have her sitting there at arm's length, beaming at him… it left him needing to take a deep breath to steady himself.

Lara showed up at their table to take their order, her eyes darting to him in question. "Are ye ready to place yer order?"

Angus tilted his head at Rowan, so she'd order. "The fish and chips, please."

Angus took Rowan's menu and set it aside behind the napkin holder. "Make that two."

Lara jotted it down, and then pinned him with a stare and a cocked eyebrow. "So, Angus, are ye not going to introduce us?"

There'd be no stemming the flow of gossip now that Lara was in the mix. At least she was young enough to not know of Rowan's mother—not that there weren't other issues to deal with. "Lara, this is Rowan Campbell. Rowan, Lara Graham, the keeper of this fine establishment."

"A pleasure. Campbell, eh? And how do ye know our dear Angus?" Lara wasn't exactly warm and inviting, but she was always a bit harsh whenever Angus came in with any woman other than his Ma or sister.

"He's a good friend." It became clear that Rowan had picked up on Lara's tone. With a smile she reached out and gave his hand a quick squeeze. "Been truly indispensable. I couldn't have made the move here without his help."

"So ye're staying then? At the Campbell cottage?"

"I am. It's a lovely area and town." Rowan gave Lara a wide smile. "And everyone's been so friendly. I know it'll feel like home in no time at all."

Angus had to bite back a laugh. Rowan had played Lara perfectly, putting an end to any escalation and diffusing the situation by calling to Lara's obligation to be hospitable. He loved that she already felt at ease. Might make it easier for her if things got difficult.

"Aye. I'm sure it will. I'll put yer order in, then." And with that, Lara was off.

Rowan was now staring at him with amusement. "Ex-girlfriend of yours?"

He barked out a laugh. "Aye, but we were just kids—still in secondary school, and it didn't last more than a few months."

Her tone was teasing, her eyes sparkling with mischief. "Well, you certainly made a lasting impression. Did you leave all the girls heartbroken?"

"Me?" He leaned forward, his elbows on the table as he closed the distance between them. "Nae, love. I was always the one nursing a broken heart."

She didn't pull away, but rather held her ground, despite the energy that seemed to spark and crackle between them, leaving the air charged. "I don't believe it, Angus Macleod."

Freckles, porcelain skin, deep red curls, and full kissable lips. By the gods, he was a goner. "Nothing but the truth, though it's all for the best."

Her eyes narrowed with curiosity. "And why's that?"

"Cause it leaves me single for when the right lass comes along." So incredibly close. He could see the flecks of brown in her green eyes, and the intelligence there. Could breathe in her scent. She smelled like the forest, like peonies and wood fires, cedar and jasmine. It left him wanting to bury his head against the curve of her shoulder.

"Is that so?" A smile tugged at her lips, but he saw her quickly get it under control.

"Aye, it is."

She sat back and picked up her napkin, folding it absent-mindedly, her eyes on what she was doing, even when she spoke. "And what if you get your heart broken again?"

"It's the chance we all take, is it not?" With her mood turning towards the serious, Angus figured a change in subject was probably best. "Ye said ye hadn't seen the stones yet. Is that correct?"

"I'm afraid I went the other way when I took my walk this morning." Her eyes then drifted past him to the crowd beyond. "Speak of the devil; there's Conall."

And no seat to be had in the entire place. Angus hoped Conall would turn around and walk away, but he knew he'd not be that lucky. His worst fears came true as Conall wandered over in their direction, looking for a table.

When Conall spotted them, Rowan gave a quick wave in response to his head nod. With a look of apology at Angus, Rowan shifted over in the booth and addressed Conall. "You're welcome to join us if you'd like. I doubt there are any available seats."

"I appreciate it." Conall slid in next to Rowan. "Angus. How ye been?"

Angus tried to swallow his annoyance, knowing full well that if not for Rowan's company, Conall would rather sit on the floor than with him. And what of the bad blood between their families? He guessed Conall was willing to put it on hold in the presence of a pretty face. At least that was something.

Angus decided he'd try his best to be civil—for Rowan's sake. "Been well. And you? Heard ye have a new dog."

"Aye. My sister left the pup with me when she took the job in Paris—though I half-suspect she left just to get away from the crazy mutt. She sends her regards, by the way." Conall stared at him as if to judge his reaction. Or was it purely to annoy him?

"I'm sure she'll enjoy Paris. It suits her." It'd been at least a year or two since he'd last seen Moira, and a good five years since their relationship ended. "As for the dog, make sure ye bring her by if she's not up to date with her vaccinations."

"She's up to date." His tone was clipped, his eyes hard.

Before they could say another word, Lara showed up at their table. "Well, I ne'er thought I'd see the day. Look at the two of ye sitting together and not killing each other. The only thing marring the vision is that ye look like two hungry dogs fighting over the same bone, despite there being plenty of others to choose from. Typical."

Conall glared at her. "Are ye going to take my order or did ye come here just to annoy us?"

Lara threw back her head and laughed. "Ye always were a feisty one." To Rowan she added, "Ye'll have to let me know if that feistiness extends into the bedroom."

"*Lara!* Quit harassing my customers and do yer job." Lara's father scowled at her from behind the counter as he pulled a pint.

"What'll ye be having then?" Lara glared at Conall, as if it was his fault she got in trouble.

"Burger and a pint, if you'd be so kind." Once Lara had gone, Conall turned his attention to Rowan. "Has Angus been showing ye around the place?"

"He has, though we've only just started." Rowan glanced over at Angus, her eyes sparkling with mischief.

"Aye, we'll head to the stones from here and then maybe wander down the coast."

"Well, if ye need anything, I'm just down the road from ye. I'd be happy to help, especially since I owe ye for Piper. I'd ne'er have caught that mutt if it weren't for yer assistance."

Rowan smiled with a casual shrug. "She found me, so I can't take all the credit, though I'll certainly keep you in mind if I find myself in need of anything."

Angus wanted to groan. He was sure Conall would love to help fulfill her needs. He could see being nice in a neighborly sort of way, but given their family history, the last thing Angus expected was for Conall to be cozying up to her.

Granted, if he had to choose someone to cozy up to, Rowan would be an excellent choice. And with that thought, he felt the earth shift below his feet and his heart quicken, knowing he was going down one slippery slope.

CHAPTER
Three

ROWAN FELT BAD that she'd invited Conall to join them, not realizing how bad things were between the two men. She was thankful they were doing their best to keep it civil, and it seemed like the tension between them had started to fade.

Conall finished the last of his burger and pint. "I appreciate ye letting me grab a seat. Rowan, it's been a pleasure."

She nodded, happy that his gruff demeanor had passed and he even seemed down right friendly.

"Angus." Conall tipped his head, tossed some money on the table and was off through the crowds.

"Shall we get going then?" When Angus pulled out his wallet she stopped him with a hand on his arm.

"Don't you dare. This is on me, you hear?" She'd be indebted to him for an eternity if he kept this up. She grabbed the check, and pulled out several bills from her wallet, leaving enough to cover the total and a generous tip.

"Only if ye let me repay ye by cooking ye dinner one of these nights." When Angus smiled at her, she had to smile back. Maybe by then she'd have a better idea as to whether she should ask Angus for help finding her father.

She could do it on her own, but he was far more familiar with the people and the area. And finding her dad was her top priority. She'd lived her entire life wondering, questioning, and beating back the insecurities that constantly threatened to creep up on her. Her mom had done her best to give her a normal childhood, but it was hard to ignore that not only was her father nowhere to be found, but her mom refused to say a word about him. There were no pictures of him, no correspondence, not even a name.

Rowan was happy to leave behind her thoughts and the crowded pub. Stepping out onto the cobblestone sidewalk, she reveled in the energy of the crisp salt air whipping around her. It left her feeling as if anything was possible.

Though she didn't want their day together to end, she knew Angus must be juggling a busy schedule. "You don't have to show me around if you're busy. I know you have patients to see."

"Nonsense. Anyone who needed seeing to was taken care of this morning, and after all these months of talking to ye online, there's nothing I want more than to spend the day showing ye the sights."

That made her smile. "You're really sweet, Angus."

"Come then. We've yet to see the stones, and the coast will be a lovely drive."

It didn't take long to get there, and would make a nice walk from the cottage. Rowan wandered down the path with Angus at her side, the circle of stones sitting off in the distance at the crest of a hill. Purple heather clung to the rocky surface like a patchwork of color dotting the fields, while the sun streaked through the clouds, painting the world in gold. It was beautiful.

With camera in hand, she paused for a moment and after a few adjustments, took several shots. "Now it's your turn."

"My turn? Very well." Angus turned towards her, and closed the distance between them, his hand outstretched to take the camera.

She handed it to him, and then leaned in to point a few things out, her body brushing against his, the feel of him solid with muscles hard and lean under casual clothing. She took a deep breath and tried to concentrate on the matter at hand—though his scent of leather and wool only made matters more difficult.

She shook her thoughts free, and did her best to ignore the catch of her pulse. "There are two settings that will affect how much light gets into the camera—your aperture and your shutter speed. If you want to focus on something in the foreground while blurring the background, you want this number here next to the f to be a small number. If you want both the foreground and background to be in focus, then you want a larger number."

"Got it. Small number for focusing on a pretty face." He played with the dials and then held the camera up, pointing it at her.

She tried to remember how to flirt back, and came up empty. Had she always been this hopeless or was it just the effect Angus had on her? Well, until she figured out how to flirt without batting her eyelashes like a total fool, she'd have to concentrate on taking pictures.

"You'll need to focus the image now." His hand went to the lens at her instruction. "That's right. Just slowly turn it until my image becomes crisp. Once you have it where you want it, gently depress the button and take the picture."

She heard the click.

"It worked." He gave her a big smile, while holding the camera out so she could see his handiwork. "I may still need a few more lessons though."

"Not bad at all." She looked up into those blue eyes, and realized he was even closer. When he brushed a stray curl from her face, a burning heat flushed her cheeks and made her pulse race. Cursing herself, she looked away and hoped he didn't notice. "Shall we head to the stones?"

He gave her a crooked smile. "Aye. Just watch your step. The rocky surface can roll underfoot, and it's far too easy to sprain an ankle."

They continued on, and before long they arrived at a circle of large stones, easily as tall as Angus at just over six feet.

It was breathtaking. Excitement bubbled within her as if the area itself vibrated with an ancient power. Perhaps it was just being in the presence of something built so long ago, or maybe it was the area and its history—but it was as if the place itself was steeped with centuries of energy from those who'd come to worship the gods of old.

They said nothing for a long time, while taking in the beauty of the stones set against a backdrop of rolling hills and heather. A calm overtook her as she breathed deep, the salt air already familiar.

She took several pictures, and then handed the camera to Angus. "Why don't you try and take one that keeps both the stones and the hills beyond in focus."

Mumbling her initial instructions under his breath, he adjusted the dial, focused the lens and took several pictures, pausing between each one to see how he did. "What do you think?"

He handed her the camera, and she took a step closer so they could both look at the pictures. She smiled while tabbing through the images. "They're very good, Angus."

"I have a good teacher." Their bodies brushed again as he glanced down at her with a sweet smile.

It would be so easy to lean in just a little more, his lips far too enticing. She was starting to think he was trouble she'd be happy to have, but she was rushing things like a virgin on prom night. He was not a distraction she had time for, even if she had no doubt he'd make it worth her while.

Forcing herself to put some distance between them, she focused on the amazing scenic views and took several more pictures. "What's that there—the stone with the hole in it?" She took several photos of it, thinking it odd.

"Ah... that'd be the lover's stone. Lover's would pass their hands through the hole and declare their undying love. It would bind them to each other as husband and wife, their marriage often consummated here under the stars. The old ways still manage to stay alive. I've heard couples still use it."

"It's incredibly romantic, if you ask me." She stepped closer and touched the stone, the surface rough and cold under her palm. "It's almost like the place is alive with energy. Like a thousand bees have been trapped just under the surface and have the place humming."

"Aye. You're sensitive to it." He placed a hand on the stone near hers. "I've often wondered if it's the place itself or the stones. I guess it matters not in the end, since they're one with each other."

Rowan breathed deeply, the crisp salt air filling her lungs as the wind swirled around her. She felt at peace here. Looking over her shoulder at Angus and deciding to be bold, she took the time to really look at him, rather than just another stolen glimpse.

He was handsome, with a casually rugged look to him. Though his hair was short in the back, the top was just a hint on the long side, allowing his nearly black locks to loosely curl with a mind all their own. Funny enough, his dark stubble held a hint of red, as if calling out to the smattering of freckles on his cheeks.

But it was his eyes that left her mesmerized. Not a light blue like most, but rather an intense aqua. They were kind. Kind and intelligent and humorous. And when he smiled, it always reached his eyes.

Maybe he was right—maybe once she settled down and got the answers she needed, then a relationship might not be completely out of the question. But not until she found her father. Until then, she'd need to stay focused on the task at hand. How could she give herself fully to another when she didn't feel whole? When she had that big ole question mark haunting her? It was no wonder one relationship after another had failed—and she liked Angus far too much to risk ruining things between them.

Needing to escape before she did something stupid, she slipped around to the other side of the rock, putting some distance between them. It was easy enough to hide behind her camera, and she could always do with some good shots.

As she wandered around the circle, Angus trailed behind her. There was a grace in his movements and a surefooted ease in his step, despite the rocky surface which kept threatening to leave her with a twisted ankle. He seemed to belong to the place, and it suited him.

He'd easily caught up to her with his long stride. "Shall we take a drive down the coast, then?"

"I'd like that a lot." Do you mind if we stop by the house first? It's getting a bit cold, and I didn't think to bring a jacket." What had been a relatively mild, if foggy, morning, turned bitter cold with a brisk wind blowing in off the ocean. Her thick sweater just wasn't cutting it, and she hadn't brought her pea coat with her.

"Aye, the weather can be finicky around here, and if ye catch yer death, my mother will have my hide for not taking proper care of ye."

They got back to the car, and minutes later were pulling down her drive.

CHAPTER Four

ANGUS NEVER FIGURED Rowan to have a temper, given that she always seemed so sweet and easygoing. So it caught him off guard when she cursed like a sailor and hopped out of the car, stalking towards the flowers someone had left on her front stoop.

He followed after her. "Rowan."

"What a bastard." She glanced at the card, cursed some more, and then grabbed the flowers. It didn't take long for her to find the rubbish bin, and toss in the roses, vase and all.

"Do I dare ask?" Angus didn't want to pry, but... bloody hell.

"Sorry about that." The words were spoken through gritted teeth as she fished around for her keys and let them in.

"Why don't ye sit and I'll get ye a drink." He steered her towards the kitchen while he grabbed the bottle of spirits and a couple of glasses. Pouring the whisky, he thought it best to distract her from the flowers and whoever sent them. "Did ye know I lived here for a short while? For about nine months while I was renovating my place."

The smallest of smiles managed to make its way onto her lips. "I was wondering how you knew where everything was stashed. Are you done with your renovations then? My mom and I did most of the work on our house, and given that it was a two-hundred-year-old farmhouse, there was a lot to do."

He settled a glass of whisky in front of her and took a seat at her side. His mind drifted to images of her wearing a plaid flannel shirt, her hair pulled back in a perky ponytail, and a tool belt hanging on her hips. Now there would be an image to behold in person. "Och, well, if ye're handy with a hammer, I'd be happy for yer expertise. I'm afraid I didn't get as much done as I'd hoped, though I sorted enough of the place to live in while I fix the rest."

"I'm happy to help, though I don't really know what I'm doing either. My mom and I sort of winged it and hoped no one would take a close look." Another small smile. She took a sip of her whisky and quickly choked on it. "This is strong."

"Aye, it can sneak up on ye if ye're not used to it." He patted her back as she coughed.

She seemed more settled, her anger quick to flare and burn out. "The flowers were from my ex. Ex-fiancé. It was what he always sent when he was in the doghouse. Red roses so dark, they're nearly black. Lying, cheating bastard."

Ah! It was no wonder she had no interest in a relationship. And here he'd been grilling her about settling down and flirting with her like a fool. Was that why she'd left home? To get away from him? "He's clearly daft, aye?"

"I was the stupid one for not seeing what was right below my nose. Anyway, it doesn't matter. I'm definitely better off without him."

"That ye are." Hoping a change of scenery might help, he gave her hand a squeeze. "Finish your drink so we can get out of here. It'll do ye good to get some fresh air and see something new."

She gently pulled her hand from his. "I appreciate it—really, I do, Angus—but I should probably finish unpacking. Maybe I can catch up with you tomorrow?"

He wanted to argue with her, to tell her she'd be better off getting out and about, rather than sitting here alone with her thoughts and her memories, mulling over what happened. Yet it wasn't his place to say it. With a weary sigh, he got to his feet and she followed suit.

"I'm only a call away. If ye need anything at all—or even just a bit of company if ye don't feel like being alone—call me. I don't care what the time, ye pick up that phone, aye?"

"I will." She then stood on her toes and, grabbing his shirt to pull him down to her level, kissed him sweetly on the cheek.

And damn if he wasn't a goner.

CHAPTER
Five

THE WIND LASHED at the windows of the cottage as Rowan tried to distract herself with work after a very long night alone, and an even longer day. She swore she wouldn't let Stephen get to her anymore, yet the flowers he'd sent were enough to bring it all back. How the hell was she supposed to start fresh if Stephen kept reminding her of her past—and her stupid mistakes? It left her wondering if she could trust her own judgment, and it made her more than a little skittish about getting into another serious relationship.

Angus was sweet—and damn sexy—but she was already growing far too attached to him, when she had more important things she needed to get done.

She blamed it all on those cursed emails. Angus had months to wear down her defenses with his humor and good will. And seeing him in person? It only made matters worse, weakening her resolve to keep her distance. Curse him.

Pushing him from her thoughts, she slid her chair away from her desk and got to her feet, her body aching in protest after too many hours of sitting. She'd spent the entire day going through the photos she'd taken, answering emails and catching up with her clients. When she finally pulled her thoughts away from her work, it was to find the day had passed her by.

It was close to dinner time, and she'd yet to get to the supermarket. Supplies in the house were running low, and with her stomach rumbling in protest, she figured she'd best do something about it. Heading for the kitchen, she grabbed the keys neatly hanging on the hook by the back door.

She smiled at that. Everything seemed to have a place, as if Angus had set everything out in an orderly fashion. It could have been the tenant before him—or her grandfather even—though she somehow doubted it was either of them. She'd seen how organized Angus kept the trunk of his car with all his supplies, and he knew precisely where everything was stashed in her home. He seemed neat and kempt, even with his unruly hair and stubble.

Shaking her head clear of him, she headed for the door while musing how he always managed to slip back into her thoughts. Stepping outside, the wind whipped her hair free from where she'd loosely pinned it back. Tucking the strands behind her ears to try and keep them from her face, she headed to the garage—an old stone building set to the side of the garden and separate from the house. Fumbling through the keys, she tried one on the lock to the doors, had it jam part way, and then tried another. The second key slipped fully into the slot and opened the lock after a quick jiggle.

The hinges squeaked as Rowan pushed open the doors and set them against the ivy covered walls so they'd be out of the way. The smell of damp and fumes had her nose wrinkling in response, yet one look at the car and her worries melted away.

She found herself smiling, despite the mood she'd been in. It was yellow and tiny, like something you'd see at the circus crammed to the ceiling with clowns. A Mini Cooper—but not the new-fangled model. It was an Austin Mini, complete with white racing stripes on the hood and additional lights in front of the grill.

She had to wonder if this too belonged to Angus. She tried to picture him squeezing his six foot plus frame into the tiny compartment, and thought if it was indeed his, it would only endear him to her further. Not some macho sports car to match a massive ego, but rather a fun car with tons of character. He had *no* reason to overcompensate—that much was clear.

She wandered over to the left side of the car and pulled open the door, immediately realizing her mistake when she found the steering wheel on the opposite side. And damn if that wasn't a stick shift poking up in the middle between the seats. She'd forgotten Angus mentioned that.

Sliding into the seat behind the wheel, she adjusted it forward and tried to recall how to drive a standard. It quickly occurred to her that the last time she'd attempted it, she'd been away at college when her friend's declared her the designated driver and tossed her the keys.

The car started up on the first try. With her hand on the shift and her feet on the break and clutch, she jerked her way out of the garage and then steeling herself, made it down the drive, pulling out onto the road with a buck. She thanked the gods there was no one else on the road as she continued to figure out the balance of gas and clutch, the engine revving in protest and lurching forward and back. She debated whether or not she was on the right side of the road, her brain completely confused as to what was right or wrong.

Finally getting the hang of it, she relaxed enough to enjoy the sun setting over the ocean. From pinks and oranges to blues and purples, the clouds streaked across the sky to catch the dying light in painted hues. It would be a straight shot into town, but before long, she'd love to take the day to go wandering about with no destination in mind. She found it the best way to get acquainted with an area and always managed to find some hidden gems along the way.

The port town of Dunmuir sat right on the water's edge with its main street cradling the harbor. Each building was a different pastel color, bright and cheery in contrast to the grey sky and turbulent ocean. Lights dotted the street and shop windows, as night slowly blanketed the area, despite it being barely half past five.

Rowan parked and then wandered down the street, taking in the shops, the storefronts painted a rainbow of pastel colors. There was even an empty store-front for lease, which sent Angus's words about selling her artwork buzzing through her brain. She'd always wanted to open a gallery, and this would be all too tempting. She peeked through the glass. It had plenty of space, a fair amount of light and was in a great location. Maybe once she'd tracked down her father. Until then, she didn't want to spread herself too thin.

Pulling herself away from the empty store and her dreams, she headed to the market and grabbed a tiny shopping cart at the entry. It was a large enough shop, given the size of the town, and seemed to stock all the essentials with a few indulgences and several locally made products. She quickly filled her basket with fruits and vegetables, picked up some free-range chicken, a bottle of wine and, unable to resist, a scrumptious looking sticky toffee pudding.

There were a few others in the shop, and it was clear they'd pegged her as someone new in town, their eyes wandering over in her direction as whispers were murmured. It was only natural that they'd be curious.

Rowan emptied her cart onto the counter, and gave the older woman a smile and a simple greeting. She said little while the woman scanned her items in, though it was hard to miss the scrutiny she was under, the woman's eyes barely leaving Rowan's face.

"Not from around here, aye?" Another item scanned.

"No, I've only just arrived. It's a lovely town though, and I'm looking forward to getting to know the area and the people." Rowan managed a sincere smile, despite the woman's blank face. Angus mentioned it might take the locals a while to warm up to her and the last thing she wanted was to get off on the wrong foot with them.

"Ye're staying then?" Eyebrows perked in question as if daring her to admit it.

"I am." Some of Rowan's smile faded, though she held the woman's gaze. She knew she was the stranger in the situation, but she refused to be intimidated. "I haven't been here long, but I already love it and look forward to making it my home. I'm surprised my mother ever left."

"Yer mother?" The woman's eyebrows shot so far up her forehead, Rowan could barely see them peeking out from under the woman's bangs. "And who would that be?"

"Iona Campbell. She moved away after college." The surprise on the woman's face caught Rowan off guard. "Did you know her?"

"Och, aye. And I wouldn't be the only one familiar with her." There was something in her tone... She then tilted her head towards the groceries. "That'll be thirty-two pounds twenty."

Rowan tried to puzzle out the woman's reaction and response to her mother's name while she paid her bill. She grabbed her things and headed out to the car, once more wondering what the hell was up. Was it just the bad blood? Or was there more to it? Angus had also been all sorts of weird when it came to discussing her mother and the past.

Maybe it was time she paid him a visit.

She gave him a quick call to make sure it'd be okay to drop in on him, and though he sounded surprised, he also seemed happy to hear from her. He gave her his address and she plugged it into her phone's GPS. Before long, she found herself turning down the drive towards an amazing home.

Part stone and part stucco, it looked like a hunting lodge, with wooden beams exposed at the roofline and large windows gracing every wall. She didn't know what condition the home had been in before Angus started his renovations, but she was damn well impressed.

She heard a dog barking inside, and before she'd even had a chance to knock, Angus pulled the door open. "I'm glad ye called, love."

"Don't know if you've eaten, but I brought dinner." She had to laugh at herself. "We just need to cook it."

"Well then, ye're in luck, since cooking is one of my specialties." He grabbed the groceries she was carrying and closed the door behind her. "Welcome to my home. The dog desperately trying to get yer attention is Astro."

"Astro, huh?" She gave the large grey shaggy mutt a good scratch, and then followed Angus to the back of the home and into the kitchen. The inside of the home left her even more impressed than the outside. "Angus, you realize this is an amazing house, right?"

"I'm glad ye like it. It's still a long way from being done, but I managed to get the important stuff out of the way—the kitchen and baths, the living room and master. I'll slowly finish up the rest once I figure out what I want to do, design-wise." He put the bags on the counter and started emptying them, as Astro watched on with curiosity. "I think we've got the makings of a decent dinner here. Why don't ye get us a glass of wine while I get started?"

"I can help cook, you know." She poked around the cupboards until she found two wine glasses.

He gave her a smile over his shoulder as he started pulling out pans. "Sit and relax, love. I've got this. Anything ye won't eat?"

"Not in this part of the world." Rowan propped herself against the island.

"That's what I like to hear." Angus pulled out a cutting board and a sharp knife, and got started on the chicken as she poured them some wine. "I have to say, I was surprised to get yer call."

"I hadn't wanted to take up any more of your time, so I spent the day catching up on business. But the woman working at the market made me think I should come talk to you." She watched him, looking for any sign that he was hiding something.

"Oh? About what?" He gave a quick glance in her direction, but was immediately back to deboning the bird. When Astro started to beg, Angus sent him to a dog bed in the corner of the kitchen.

"The woman working at the shop gave me a funky look when she found out who my mother was. And the last time I saw you, you sort of skirted around the issue." She bit her lip, wondering what the hell was up. "Is there something I should know? 'Cause I really don't like being left in the dark."

He stopped cutting for a moment, and then started up again. "Truth is, I know precious little, and frankly it's not my place to speculate."

"Angus, please." It was bad enough she was a stranger town. But to not know something about her family when everyone else did, left her on edge. "I hate hearing the whispers when I don't know what they're talking about."

"It's probably nothing, aye? The locals are going to be curious, especially in such a small town. They'll want to know why ye moved here, and if they recognize yer name, then they might wonder about yer ma. Don't go reading more into it than there really is."

"What about the bad blood you mentioned. Maybe it has to do with that?" She let out a weary sigh as frustration crept into her bones and knotted her muscles.

He finished boning the chicken and tossed into the pan, before cleaning his work area and scrubbing his hands clean. When he turned back to her, she could see the internal debate running through that gorgeous head of his. However, he didn't say anything, and instead pulled out more ingredients, knives, and cutting boards.

She had to smile. "Are you ignoring me, Angus?"

"It'd be impossible to ignore someone as lovely as yerself, my dear." He chopped at some mushrooms while giving her a flirty smile.

"Angus, please." She reached out and touched his arm, needing to feel like he was on her side—especially since it was becoming clear that she'd need his help if she had any hope of finding her father. The locals trusted

Angus—and she'd garnered nothing more than stares and whispers. It was doubtful they'd answer any of her questions, and though she might eventually finagle it, she couldn't wait that long. Hell, they'd probably still see her as a stranger a decade from now.

"Aye, I suppose I can tell ye what I know, though it's not much." With a sigh, he gave the chicken a quick stir, added a few more ingredients, and then dropped some pasta into the boiling water. "It's my understanding that yer mother and Conall's father were engaged to be married when yer ma called it off. I'm not sure under what circumstances they split up, but I'm sure that's what's fueling the whispers from the locals. Back then, anything at all was fodder for gossip and a big scandal."

Maybe that's all it was, though her mother had never mentioned any sort of engagement—or anything else for that matter. "I guess that could be it."

"Aye, love. No point in getting yer knickers in a twist o'er nothing at all—especially by today's standards." He tilted his head towards a cabinet. "Mind getting out a few dishes?"

She set two plates on the counter and then dug around for some silverware as Angus plated something that smelled absolutely incredible. Good looking, smart, sweet—*and* he could cook. He must have dead bodies in the basement or something.

"Hope ye like chicken marsala. Grab yer plate and wine, and we'll eat by the fire in the sitting room."

Astro was quick to his feet at the first sign the food would be moving locations, and followed after them. The sitting room left her impressed once more, with its cathedral ceilings, a massive stone fireplace flanked by a bay of windows, while exposed wood beams lined the roofline.

Once they settled in on the sofa, she took a bite of her meal and was blown away by the flavors. Rich and creamy, the mushrooms and wine played off the chicken and roasted garlic, while the pasta balanced out the dish. "Damn, this is good, Angus. Is there anything you can't do?"

"Well, I do try my hardest." He gave her a wink and a smile, before twirling some linguine onto his fork. "Just don't ask me to do any gardening. My Da's the gardener in our family. He could make anything grow, no matter what the conditions. I, on the other hand, couldn't manage to grow weeds if my life depended on it. And forget dancing. Having me as yer dance partner could easily land ye in a wheelchair. How about yerself? What are ye absolutely miserable at doing?"

"Do you really have time for that sort of list?" She had to laugh as she thought of the things she always managed to muck up. "I think of myself as being very good at a handful of things, and horrible at the rest."

He sat back and gave her a teasing smile. "I don't believe ye. Not one bit."

"All right, maybe it's not that bad, as long as you don't ask me to sing or play an instrument—despite the collection I've managed to accumulate. And I can't garden either. Or knit, no matter how many classes I take."

"Och, well, if ye can't garden, sing and knit while here in the highlands, then ye'll ne'er manage to find yerself a husband. Good thing I'm willing to overlook those tragic faults." He tilted his head towards her with a wink.

She burst out laughing. "You know, one of these days some woman's going to take your offer seriously, and you'll find yourself in a pickle."

"Och, love, ye don't think I'd proposition just anyone, do ye?" He feigned mock horror. "I have standards, my dear."

"You're trouble, Angus—and I know better. But you're also sweet, smart and funny. I'll give you that."

He gave her hand a squeeze. "It's only because ye bring out the best in me."

Maybe now would be a good time to ask for his help. She could put it off a bit longer, but she suspected she wouldn't get far without him. Better to not waste any time.

"Angus, I have a huge favor to ask, and I feel horrible that I'm bugging you again after all you've done." She took a deep breath and tried to ignore her racing heart and the twist of her stomach. "The truth is it's the reason I came to Scotland, and I really don't think I can do this without you."

"What is it, love? Ye have me worried." His brow furrowed as he shifted towards her, his eyes locked on hers.

She let out a weary sigh. "I want to find out who my father is."

CHAPTER
Six

NGUS WASN'T SURE what she was going to ask, but her request caught him off guard. "I don't understand—do ye not know yer father?"

She shook her head, her eyes shimmering in the firelight. "No. Nothing. No photos. No letters. Not even a name."

He heard the catch in her voice and it left his heart aching for her. As close as his family was, he couldn't imagine what she was going through. It'd be bad enough to grow up without a father in her life, but to not even know who he is… Angus couldn't imagine what that would be like.

"Did yer mother not leave ye any information before passing?" When she shook her head no, he felt her despair. "Do ye have any clue as to who he may be? Any place to start looking?"

"There's a bank account in my name that's had deposits made into it annually—and generous amounts at that. I tried to get information on who's making the deposits, but it's listed as a law firm, and they won't give me any information." She sat back with a sigh. "The firm—it's here in Scotland, but I have nothing else to go on."

"Do ye think ye're ma was pregnant when she called off her engagement?" Angus didn't like bringing it up, but skirting around the issue because it might be rude certainly wouldn't help her any. "It might be the reason they split. I hate to say it, love, but if they weren't rushed off to the altar, then it's doubtful he was the father."

"I didn't know about the engagement and she never said why she left Scotland, but it sort of makes sense. If she'd been engaged to Conall's father and ended up pregnant by another guy, it'd be a good enough reason to fuel the bad blood between the families. It would also explain why she moved away. It'd have to be something pretty significant since my grandmother had already passed when my mom was young, and she'd be leaving my grandfather all alone."

He could just imagine. "Don't forget, things were a bit different back then. This was what? Twenty-six years ago, right? Out of wedlock pregnancies—and worse, pregnancies that didn't end with a wedding— weren't exactly looked upon too kindly."

"That would probably account for the whispers and stares, not to mention the woman behind the counter—she said something about not being the only one *familiar* with my mother. It was the way she said it—like there was some sort of innuendo." Rowan shook her head and scoffed. "Makes sense now."

"Listen, love. Ye can't pay them any heed." His chest was tight with a brewing anger, his muscles tense. She'd barely been here more than a few days, and already she'd been made to feel uncomfortable. "Don't let them get to ye."

"Oh, I won't." For a moment, she looked like she was mulling something over, but then a sly smile tugged at her lips as if she'd come to some sort of decision. "And I want to make sure they know that they can't get rid of me so easily. I'm not going to be intimidated or run out of town."

A smile like that looked far too mischievous to be any good. "What are ye up to, Rowan?"

"I'm taking your advice." She beamed at him, and though he was happy to see her worries fade, the sinking feeling in the pit of his stomach made him nervous.

"What advice would that be?" He ran through all the things he'd said to her, wondering what she'd latched onto, and what she could possibly be thinking.

"I'm going to open a gallery in town." Her grin was now joined by a sparkle in her eyes. "It's something I've always wanted to do, and it'll give people a chance to get to know me."

"Och, aye. They'll get to know ye, all right." He laughed, relieved it was nothing so troublesome. She was going to take the town by storm, and they wouldn't know what hit them. "So what will ye do about yer father?"

"I guess that's where I could use some help." She bit her bottom lip, her eyes locked on his. "Since my mom never spoke about her past, I don't really know where to start. And after today? I'm wondering if anyone will talk to me, even if they have information I could use."

She was right to worry. Angus knew they wouldn't give up any information to someone they didn't know—not that they wouldn't gossip to each other, given half the chance. "Let me see if my Ma knows what happened. She might be able to help."

In her excitement, she grabbed his arm, her touch making his heart pound all the harder. "Do you really think she would?"

"Aye, love. I do."

Angus kept himself busy with work throughout the morning, though his mind kept wandering back to Rowan. Unfortunately, he had quite a bit of travelling to do, and driving did nothing to distract him.

He'd thought of asking her to join him, but didn't want to suffocate the poor girl with his attentions. She'd made it quite clear that she didn't have any desire to start any sort of romantic involvement, and though he hadn't given up hope of changing her mind, he did understand that she had a lot going on in her life, and a relationship would only complicate matters.

That was fine. He was fairly patient, and happy to give her all the space she needed. It's not like he was going anywhere.

Not far from his parents' home, he decided to swing by to see if his mother was in. If Rowan was going to go digging into her mother's past, then he thought he should give his Ma a head's up. Not that his mother wouldn't help any way she could, but the issue might be a touchy one and he didn't want her to be caught off guard.

He let himself in and wandered towards the kitchen, knowing he'd find his parents there at this time of the day. "Hey, Ma."

"Now there's a pleasant surprise. Hadn't been expecting ye." She wiped her hands on a dish towel, and leaned in so he could kiss her cheek. "The kettle's boiled if ye want a cuppa."

"Aye. Can I get ye one?"

"May as well." She smiled over her shoulder at him, while throwing some spices into a pot she had simmering on the stove, the smell of it heavenly. Some sort of meat stew if he had to guess, the scent of wine, thyme and bay leaf heady in the air, the heat from the pot fogging the windows.

He poured them each a cup of tea and doctored them both with milk and sugar, before grabbing the biscuits. "Where's Da?"

"Out with Callum MacCraigh, though he'll be back in time for dinner. Will ye be staying?" She sat at the table and took her tea from him.

He should stay, if only to keep him from wandering over to Rowan's. "Nae... I've got some work I need to get done."

"So how is the lass? Have ye gotten her settled in?" Her eyes lingered on her youngest, but they were always too knowing, despite being kind, and they missed nothing, especially where her children were concerned.

"Aye, she seems to be adjusting just fine, though I'm not sure how others are adjusting to her." He let out a weary sigh, before taking a sip of his tea. "I know ye warned me they'd be hard on her, but bloody hell. I don't know what happened with her Ma, but people are giving her looks and whispering behind her back. I worry things will only get worse."

His mother frowned, her gaze on her tea. "After so many years, ye'd think they'd leave it be. I was hoping they'd have forgotten, but people have a hard time letting things go." When she swore under her breath in Gaelic, Angus knew just how angry she was.

"There's more, Ma. She's looking for her father. She doesn't know who he is, and wants to speak to ye about what happened."

His mother looked away with a shake of her head. "Och, Angus. She can't go looking for him. I mean it. I don't know who her father is, but I can tell ye now, she can't go looking for him. It just won't do."

It was like he'd been punched in the gut. It was the last thing he'd expected her to say. "Ma... ye can't mean that. It's the reason she's come all this way. It feels like she's got her entire life on hold. She won't ever be able to move forward until she has some answers."

What the hell had happened all those years ago? He dunked a few biscuits into his tea and ate them in two bites. Repeating it a few more times, the ritual of sitting there in the kitchen with a cuppa, slowly calmed his nerves. "She's already run into Conall Stewart, and I don't know what the hell's up with him, but his normally cantankerous mood has suddenly turned chipper in her presence."

"Perhaps he's putting their family's issues to the side. If the girl looks anything like her mother, then I could see why he might be smiling, aye?"

Her gaze held his as if looking to see if he'd fallen under the same spell. It had him pursing his lips and trying not to blush. "Still... I don't like that he's done such an abrupt turnaround. Makes me wonder what he's up to."

"Och, Angus. He's not a bad lad, so don't let him bother ye. And I'll tell ye now, he's the least of our problems if Rowan's going to go looking for her father." Her lips pursed into a thin line, her brow furrowed. Angus had never seen her looking so worried.

"Ma… she needs to do this."

"Aye, son. I know. But I swear, I'll ne'er forget how shaken Iona was after coming home from university. She made me promise to not go digging into who the father was. Said it was for my own good—and I believed her, scared as she looked. I don't know who she got involved with, but if Rowan's going to go looking for the man, then it leaves me worried. There was a reason Iona never returned home and left her father on his own. And to not tell Rowan who her father is, even when she was sick… there had to be a reason, Angus." She let out a weary sigh, her brow furrowed and her jaw tight. "It could put her in danger, son—and though I don't have any answers for ye, I can tell ye that Iona's fear was real."

"So, what am I to do? I told her I'd help her." Angus's head was spinning and his heart was heavy. He knew what finding her father meant to Rowan, and didn't know if he could stand in her way.

"Above all else, ye need to keep her safe, Angus. For Iona's sake. Her mother was like my sister, aye? Ye do what ye must to keep her from finding him—to keep her from harm. Even if she'll hate ye for it. I'm sorry, son. I really am. I know ye like the lass and want to help her, but it's for her own good." With sadness in her eyes, she patted his arm and got to her feet.

"Ma… I don't know if I can do that. Ye know I'm not any good at lying, and doesn't she have a right to know?" Though he could normally lie without anyone ever knowing, it usually didn't take long before he confessed it all, unable to deal with the burden of his lies.

She gave him a worried smile. "Aye. I know this will be hard on ye. Ye always had too guilty a conscience." Her smile then faded to concern. "But it's for her own good, Angus, and ye'll need to do all ye can to make sure she doesn't find him or start asking too many questions. Make sure she doesn't go looking for him. Find a way to distract her or keep her busy. And if she does go looking, make sure she doesn't find anything, aye? It might be the only way to keep her safe."

He groaned, his heart and head filled with dread. "Aye, Ma. I'll try my best."

She nodded, worry lining her face. "Let her know she's invited to dinner. Tomorrow, if it's convenient for her. If ye could pass on the invitation, I'd appreciate it."

"Aye, Ma. I'll let her know, though I can tell ye now, she'll ask about her father." What a bloody mess. He finished his tea and put his cup in the sink, before kissing his mother on the cheek. "Tell Da I stopped by."

He'd need to see Rowan to tell her about dinner with his parents, though what he'd do about helping her search for her father, he hadn't a clue. This was the last thing he needed, especially the way he felt about her. Already his heart beat faster to know he'd soon be with her again—and the guilt had his stomach in knots.

The friendship they'd developed via email and the attraction he felt for her was only solidified when she closed the distance between them with her move. He knew he shouldn't grow so attached to her, yet he couldn't help himself. She was even more tempting in person with those fiery locks, green eyes, and luscious curves.

And now? He'd be putting everything at risk to try and keep her safe. By the gods, she'd hate him if she ever found out he was keeping her from finding her father.

Driving by the port, he caught sight of his little yellow mini—not many of those around. That meant Rowan was in town. He parked, and with a quick look up and down the road, spotted her stepping out of a shop a few blocks up.

Heading down the road towards him, a smile sprung to her lips—and by the gods, he was a goner. The fact that *he* could make her smile like that, the fact that the smile dancing on her lips and the light in her eyes were because she'd seen him… it only reinforced how he felt about her, how she made him feel.

She closed the distance between them, giving him a quick hug, and in European fashion, a peck on the cheek, his pulse tripping to have her so close. "Fancy meeting you here."

"The yellow Mini's hard to miss, and since it's the only one in the area, I figured ye couldn't be far behind." He leaned back on his old ride, stretching his long legs out in front of him. "I spoke to my Ma—she'd like to have ye over for dinner if ye're available tomorrow."

"I'd love to..." When she bit her lip and her brow furrowed, Angus knew what would be coming next. "Did you ask her? About my father?"

That put a damper on his enthusiasm. How the hell was he going to deter her when it was the only thing on her mind? It'd be impossible to keep her from looking for her father. "Aye, lass. I asked, and she'd love to help, but unfortunately, she doesn't really have a whole lot of information for ye. I'm sorry, aye? Yer ma didn't give her any details."

She nodded and reached out to give his hand a squeeze. "Still. Maybe she'll recall something once we start talking. And one way or another, it'll be a start, even if it's to cross her off my list of people I've spoken to."

He heard the emotion in her voice and saw the sparkle of unshed tears in her eyes, unable to imagine what an emotional journey it must be for her. It must be so difficult to try and stay positive and keep looking.

His mother said Iona seemed scared before leaving for the States. The question was why? His Ma might be wrong, of course, but could he take that risk? And did that mean Rowan might be stirring things up when they should be left alone? Or was the threat long gone?

"Aye, love. It'll all work out for the best." He managed a smile and was happy to see her eyes clear up, though he already felt horrible that he wasn't being completely honest with her.

"I've got good news." She bit her lip again. "I bought the shop, so I can open a gallery and studio."

"Bought it? I thought it was for lease?" Bloody hell, the lass worked fast. It'd be impossible to keep her out of trouble.

She cocked her head and a smile tugged at her full, kissable lips. "It was, but when I asked if I could purchase it instead, the owner was happy to sell—and for a good price too. I wanted to make a statement. I want people to know that I'm going to make this my home, and I won't be driven away by their whispers and cold shoulders."

"Have people been giving ye a hard time?" His brow furrowed at the thought, and he now found himself worrying about how the locals would respond to her buying the shop. If things escalated, he'd not be happy.

"I can deal with the locals, Angus. Let them talk all they want."

"Rowan, I wish ye had waited a bit. Ye probably haven't even recovered from jetlag and ye've already bought a place." He wanted to be supportive, but she had him worried, damn it. Did she not think things through?

"And?" Her tone held an edge to it.

"Listen, lass. The decision's yers to make, and no one else's. I'm not saying it was a good move or bad, I just think ye're moving a bit quick, is all."

"Well, you're right—it is my decision, and I've made it."

When she crossed her arms in front of her chest, he knew she was annoyed with him. "So ye have. How about ye let me buy ye a pint and some dinner to congratulate ye on yer recent purchase and make it up to ye for speaking out of turn."

He could see her debating whether or not to be angry with him. She then gave him a sideways grin, her red hair catching in the wind coming off the sea. "You're just lucky you're cute, and I know no one else in town."

"Aye, a good thing indeed." He tried to lighten the mood. "And a good thing I'm the one buying ye dinner. People might start to talk if you're always the one paying my way."

"And what exactly would they be saying?" She narrowed her eyes in question, a smile quirking at her lips.

"Nothing much at all—except that ye might have yerself a handsome and dashing boy toy." He could barely keep a straight face, and it felt good to push his worries aside, even if it was just for a moment.

The tension melted between them as she barked out a laugh. "You're lucky I have a sense of humor and I don't tend to hold onto my anger. Not that you don't have a right to your opinion… it's just that I want you to be happy for me."

"Och, love. I am." He shifted himself off the car and stood, stuffing his hands in his jean pockets to keep from reaching out to take her hand. "So, where would ye like to go?"

"The pub's fine." She slipped her hand around his arm and beamed a smile up at him as they wandered down the road. "I can tell you all about my plans for the gallery."

"I'd love to hear them." He looked down at her, his heart racing to have her at his side, despite his mother's warning niggling at the back of his thoughts, keeping him from fully enjoying his time with her.

They grabbed a booth by a window, the pub nowhere near as busy as it had been the last time they were there. It was too late for lunch and too early for dinner. The only ones there were those nursing a pint and the ones who never left except at closing.

Lara came to take their order. "Back so soon? Must be my lucky day."

Angus ignored her sarcastic glare. "How someone hasn't snapped ye up for his own astonishes me on a daily basis, my dear."

"Ye've always been cheeky." Lara playfully slapped his arm and then turned to Rowan. "So ye really are staying? *Here* of all places? Why is beyond me."

"As a matter of fact, I just bought the shop a few doors down." Rowan beamed at her.

"Lovely. My day just keeps getting better." She tilted her head towards the menus. "Do ye know what ye want then?"

They placed their order. Once Lara was gone, he leaned forward. "She's really not that bad once ye get used to her."

"I'm sure that'd be the case if I weren't here with you. But she's seen us together twice, and though we're nothing more than friends, she doesn't see it that way because you're her ex." She shrugged her shoulders, a knowing smile on her lips. "It's just how women work."

He ignored how much it bothered him that she still didn't think of him as anything more than a friend. "So tell me about the shop. Ye said it was just a few doors down from here? The internet café?"

"That's the one." Her smile had him forgetting about his worries. "Don't suppose you know of any good contractors?"

"Och, I can probably help ye with most of yer projects. What did ye have in mind?" It'd be a good way to keep an eye on her. Between the locals taking their sweet time to warm up to her, Rowan's impulsive side, and trying to keep her from finding her father, it'd be a miracle if they managed to avoid trouble.

"Angus… I don't mind hiring someone. You're busy with your own stuff and besides, I know you aren't too happy about my purchase."

"Listen, love… I'm happy to help, and truth is, I'm glad ye bought the place. It just caught me off guard is all." It wasn't entirely a lie. He knew that by making such a purchase, she'd be less likely to pack her bags and leave—and for that he was grateful.

"Are you sure that's it?"

"Aye, love. As for hiring someone, I have time, and I'd be happy to do it. Most days, I'm done with work by mid-afternoon, and it'd keep me busy while I figure out what to do with my remaining projects." They paused their conversation for a moment as Lara slid their food onto the table. "So what needs doing? Tell me yer plans, love."

"I'll do even better—let's eat and then we'll head over and I'll show you."

CHAPTER
Seven

"**G**IVEN THE SIZE of the check I wrote out, the owners were happy to give me the keys despite the papers still waiting for the final steps in processing." Rowan hadn't really touched the money in her secret bank account until now, and though it was a relatively large purchase, she thought it would be a good investment.

She unlocked the door with a jiggle of the key, and then pushed it open, excitement bubbling within her. The space was wide and open, with good light and plenty of windows. A fresh coat of cream paint—or taupe— would keep the walls neutral so as not to compete with the artwork.

There was a long wooden bar running parallel to the far wall, and though she had every intention of making use of the professional espresso machine, she'd likely get rid of the bar—or better yet, convert it to a display for small items, by adding glass to the front and shelving within.

Track and spot lighting would have to be added to help showcase the works, and then maybe the back area could be converted to a studio.

"So… what do you think?" She looked over at Angus, hoping he'd like it as much as she did. It had been a rather impulsive buy, but it felt right and it was a lifelong dream.

"With a bit of work, I think it'll be grand." He stepped away from her side, wandering about while taking it in. She could see the ideas churning in his head. "Some lights along the ceiling."

"And some spot lights strategically placed from below."

"Aye. Something plain on the walls."

"So it won't compete with the artwork." She smiled. He was having the same thoughts she was.

"A desk in the corner so you can work when it gets slow."

"And a studio out the back. Maybe hold classes in the evenings. A 'bring a friend, a bit of wine and learn to paint' sort of thing. Might even get a few potter's wheels and a kiln."

He looked at her, surprise registering on her face. "Do ye also do pottery then?"

"Actually, it's my first love, though I've experimented with just about every medium. Started working on the wheel when I was in high school and continued it in college, though it was impossible to keep up once I started travelling. Photography became a good alternative since it's far more portable. But now? Why not? I've got the space in the back and I could also give lessons, not to mention it'd be one more thing to sell in the gallery."

"Well, ye have yer first student then. I've always wanted to learn. It could be our little barter—I'll help ye with everything but the electrical, and in turn, ye can teach me how to make pottery."

He gave her a genuine smile, but she had to wonder… "It's not because you saw the movie *Ghost*, is it?"

His eyebrows perked up in question, his face bland. "I wouldn't know what ye're talking about, my dear."

Rowan put on one outfit after another, not quite sure what to wear to dinner, her nerves getting more frayed with each clothing change. Not only was she meeting Angus's family for the first time, but she'd also be meeting her mother's best friend—and maybe, just maybe, she'd get enough answers to start the search for her father.

Would jeans be too casual if paired with a pretty sweater and heels? Maybe. A dress? She didn't have a whole lot, since she'd been forced to cull most of her wardrobe before moving. Not to mention it was pretty damn cold out.

Ah! She pulled out a finely knit sweater-dress with a scooped cowl neck in a pretty smoke color. Digging around, she found a pair of oatmeal tights and coupled them with a pair of knee-high boots in soft chocolate brown leather. Perfect. She'd be casual but elegant, and most importantly, comfortable.

She checked the time and then finished getting ready. Angus had insisted on picking her up, since it'd be easier than trying to give her directions to his parents' home. Probably for the best, since she'd likely get lost or drive off a cliff while trying to stay on the correct side of the road.

Angus was on time, and she found it difficult to keep her excitement at bay. Though Angus's mom might not have a whole lot of information to give her, Rowan just needed enough to get her search started.

Grabbing her bag and the bottle of wine she'd bought, she opened the door before he had a chance to knock and beamed up at him. "Ready."

He took a step back and gave a low whistle. "Wow... ye look... amazing."

Relief washed over her. "Thanks. I wasn't quite sure what to wear, and well... I want your parents to like me."

"Och, ye could show up wearing a sack and they'd still love ye, lass."

She then realized Angus was wearing a kilt—coupled with a pair of Doc Martens and a comfy sweater. And damn if her pulse didn't get erratic. There was nothing she liked more than a man in a kilt, especially when they wore it well. Even better when it was kept casual. Her smile refused to be tamed. "Nice... boots."

He looked down and then gave her a crooked smile. "Aye. The kilt. My Da likes us all to be kilted for any dinner with guests. He's sort of old-fashioned that way."

"Well, you won't hear any complaints from me." She was grateful when a cool breeze hit her flaming cheeks as they headed towards his car. Though she had no time for a relationship, she told herself it was perfectly fine to enjoy the view. And what a view it was. A man in a kilt made her all sorts of hot and bothered. Good thing her nerves were enough to distract her from the effects of her non-existent love life.

The drive to his parents' home seemed relatively short, distracted as she was by Angus's banter and her nerves. When they pulled down the drive, she took a deep breath to try and calm herself. So much hinged on what she found out tonight.

"Hey..." Angus gave her hand a squeeze. "It'll be all right, love."

All her uncertainties seemed to wash over her at once. "And what if it isn't? This is my only hope, Angus. I know not to expect much, but I need *something* to go on—something to take me to the next clue. 'Cause I can't stand not knowing anymore. It feels like it's all coming to a head, and I'm going to lose it if I don't get some resolution."

He let out a weary sigh. "Rowan... what if he doesn't want to be found?"

"Don't you think I realize that? It's not like he hasn't had twenty-six years to make contact. Yet he hasn't. And you know what? I don't care. I just want a name and a face to go with it. Do you know what it's like to live with such a big question mark in your life? Everything feels unsettled. Nothing's at peace." She then scoffed. "It's no wonder Stephen went looking elsewhere. He always said I had one foot out the door."

He brushed her cheek, but she could feel a coiled tension in his touch. "He was nothing but an arse, love. *He* cheated on *you*. How is that yer fault?"

"I could have been there more. And not just physically, either. Even when I wasn't travelling, I held him at arm's length."

Angus let out a deep breath, and then brushed a stray a stray curl from her eyes, his fingers lingering. "No matter what—it doesn't excuse what he did. If he wasn't happy, he could have broken it off."

"I just want to—*need to*—find my father. I'll be fine then. I'll be whole." She blinked back tears, refusing to get all weepy and emotional, especially when she'd be heading in for dinner. The last thing she needed was to look like she'd been crying, her eyes bloodshot and lids puffy. With several deep breaths, she got a hold of herself. "We should go in."

"Are ye sure?" He looked so worried.

"You're a sweet man, Angus." She leaned forward and gave him a quick peck on the cheek. "Now let's get going before they start wondering what we're up to."

"Och, well, if we're going to give them something to wonder about, then shouldn't we at the very least be doing something awfully depraved while out here?"

She shook her head with a laugh, amazed at how he could melt her worries away with his humor. "You're so bad, Angus."

"Aye, love. Bad to the bone."

She found him looking at her, his gaze holding hers, the air between them charged. She could easily kiss him, then and there—and if she was reading him right, the same thought was crossing his mind at that very moment. It'd be so easy to just lean in a little more, to brush her lips against his. Yet her racing pulse had her breaking away, not wanting to muck things up between them. With the moment gone, she gave him an uneasy smile and made her escape, leaving him to follow.

He took her hand as he led her up the walkway. The house was traditional in style, not too unlike her mother's cottage, but much larger in size. Angus didn't knock, but rather opened the door and wandered into the sitting room, where his father was sitting by the fire, reading a book. "Da."

"Och, there ye are." Hamish Macleod got to his feet. Nearly as tall as Angus, Rowan could see the similarities not only in their height but their unruly curls and bright blue eyes.

"This here is Rowan." Angus ran a comforting hand down her back, making her grateful to have him right there by her side.

"The name's Hamish. It's a pleasure to finally meet ye." When he gave her a hearty handshake and a smile that reached his eyes, the butterflies in her stomach settled a little. Just like Angus, his father was tall and handsome—and like she'd been warned, kilted too.

Feeling more at ease, she felt some of the tightness and anticipation in her chest slip free. "The pleasure's mine."

A petite woman walked into the room behind them. "There ye are. Rowan…" Angus's mom, Anne, took both Rowan's hands in hers and gave them a squeeze, not letting go, her eyes sparkling with emotion. "Ye look so much like yer Ma did back in the day. I was so sorry to hear of her passing."

Rowan blinked back tears, not wanting to get emotional in front of everyone, but having a hard time of it. She forced a smile to her lips. "I know she missed you, even if she seldom talked about home."

"Why don't ye come into the kitchen and keep me company while I finish up dinner." Leaving the men behind, they headed to the kitchen. "Grab yerself a seat. I'm just waiting for the apple pie to finish baking. We can have that after dinner with our tea."

"Is there anything I can do to help?" She hated sitting there while others worked.

She took a seat near Rowan at the kitchen table. "Och, no, love. The pie's the only thing left, and there's nothing to do for it but wait."

Unsure of how much time they'd have alone to discuss her father, Rowan decided now was as good a time as any. Her pulse picked up its pace, and her breath quickened as she fought through her unease. "Did Angus mention that I want to speak to you?"

"Aye, he did, though I'm not sure I'll have many answers for ye, my dear."

"I'm looking for my father—do you know who he is?"

Anne's demeanor slumped as she looked at Rowan with sadness in her eyes. "No, dear. Yer mother ne'er did say. I'll admit, it was a bit of a sore spot between us. We'd been the best of friends since we were bairns, and I couldn't understand why she wouldn't tell me about him. I knew she must have had her reasons, and I eventually came around. The circumstances were hard... she was engaged to another lad, aye?"

"Was my father local, then? When did she become pregnant?" She needed information she didn't already have.

"No, he wasn't from around here, that I was aware of. She'd been away at university when it happened, so I can only assume it was a lad she'd met during her studies, though he could easily be from anywhere. She left for the states as soon as she could—would have been about four months pregnant with ye." Anne let out a deep breath. "I know ye want to know yer father, but I'm afraid there's little to point the way. Bit of a wild goose chase."

Rowan's mind raced through the possibilities. She could see her mother, young and independent, walking across campus to class, a handsome guy at her side. They wouldn't be living in a vacuum. "Someone must know—even if it's no more than who she was hanging out with. I know she lived on campus—she'd let that slip one day. Maybe her roommate met him—or perhaps he called. Did she ever mention her roommate's name?"

"I'm sure she did on more than one occasion, though I'm afraid my memory is failing me after all these years." She put a gentle hand on Rowan's arm. "I'm so sorry I'm not being much help."

"I know it's been ages since it happened, and I appreciate you trying to help. And now that I know it happened while she was in college, I'm hoping I can track down a few more leads. I can't thank you enough—already, it's far more than I had to start with." Once more, Angus and his family were there to help her. She couldn't imagine trying to do it all on her own, and having this connection to her mom was priceless. "I truly appreciate everything you and your family have done for me. I couldn't have made the move here without Angus."

Though it wasn't a lot to go on, Rowan at least knew her next step would be tracking down the people who knew her mother while she was in school. Teachers, advisors, friends, and most importantly, her mom's roommate. It finally felt like she was getting somewhere with her search, even if she was still a long way from finding her father.

Anne pulled her from her thoughts. "Yer mother was like the sister I never had, and I hope ye know, ye're like family. I would do anything I could to keep ye safe and see ye happy."

Anne's words struck at her very heart, filling it with hope. It was as if she was no longer alone in her quest. She'd tried her best to manage on her own, tried to stay strong. For the first time since her mother's death, she felt someone lighten her load and walk by her side. And it wasn't just Anne, but Angus. Feeling like she could finally take a moment to exhale—like she could dare hope to find her father—she let loose all she'd been holding back and let her tears come as Anne held her close in a motherly embrace.

She managed to get a hold of herself before long, not wanting to be an emotional mess. She swiped at her eyes with a smile and a laugh. "I think I needed that."

"Och, we all need a cry from time to time, and I suspect ye'd been holding that one in for far too long." She got to her feet and pulled out the pie, setting it aside to cool. "Now, give us a hand getting dinner to the table. I'm sure the lads are feeling like they've gone days without being fed—ne'er mind that they eat from morn until night, and barely stop long enough to take a breath."

"That was… *amazing*. My compliments." Rowan sat back in her seat, unable to eat another bite and in a damn good mood. From the pork loin wrapped in bacon and filled with onion and apple stuffing, to the apple pie topped with fresh cream, and everything in between, each bite had been a burst of flavor.

"I'm glad to hear ye enjoyed it." Anne got to her feet to clear the dishes, but Angus put a hand on her arm.

"Sit, Ma. I'll take care of it." He got to his feet and Rowan joined him. Together with just a trip or two, they had the dishes in the sink, and the food on the counter. "She'll pack it all away the way she wants—and will likely send us both home with some of it, lest we starve left to our own devices."

"Hey, you might be managing just fine, but I've yet to figure out the Aga." She hadn't told him of her attempt to bake a casserole. It had taken her three hours to get it to cook through. "And now I see where you learned to cook."

He leaned back on the counter, his long bare legs stretched out in front of him, his kilt all too… enticing. She knew she was staring—looking him up and down like a construction worker eyeballing a blonde in a red clingy dress cut way too short and far too low. Even her breath was coming in shallow spurts, leaving her light-headed. And in the good mood she was in? Anything and everything seemed possible.

"Might have to come over and give ye a few cooking lessons." His gaze took her in with a keen interest, his eyes all too intelligent and missing nothing, the room suddenly feeling too hot and too small.

She must be blushing, staring, and she'd likely add stammering to that list in just a moment. The lack of oxygen from those cursed shallow breaths was making her want to lean up against him for support—amongst other things.

And that kilt. Surely, he must know what a kilt and Docs did to a girl.

He took her hand and slowly pulled her to him so that she nestled between his legs, leaning against him. By the gods, she wanted him—and it was clear he knew it, if his slow smile and the amusement in his eyes were anything to go by.

Then it changed—amusement was replaced by raw hunger and passion, and he looked ready to devour her, his gaze intense as he took her in, the tension in his muscles coiled tight. Gone was the sweet Angus she knew, replaced by a hunter. He slipped one hand into her hair and fisted it as his arm wrapped around her waist and pinned her to him. He took her in a moment more as her breath caught in her chest and then like a beast let loose, his lips were on hers, taking, tasting, pulling her in. Her world was tipped upside down as she was left clinging to him and their kiss deepened towards something feral, ancient, primal.

Just as she lost herself in him completely, so that everything else dropped away, so all that mattered was the two of them in that moment, he slowed his kisses. Her heart pounded against her ribs as the aftershocks worked their way through her entire body, leaving her barely able to stand as her knees threatened to buckle.

All she could do was try to breathe—and ignore the bothered heat pulsing through her body, begging for release. When she finally thought she might manage a few words, it became clear the oxygen had yet to make it to her brain. "Do you kiss all the girls like that?"

"Only the pretty ones." His lips tugged into a crooked smile that had her wanting an instant replay of the kiss she'd remember for a lifetime.

By the time they said goodbye to Angus's parents and hopped in the car to head home, Rowan's doubts were niggling their way into her brain, leaving her to wonder just what she was doing with Angus. She really did like him, especially if there were kisses like that to be had. But it could also be a major mistake that would be difficult to take back and recover from.

"Ye're thinking so loud, I can hear ye all the way over here." He reached out and gave her hand a squeeze. "I shouldn't have kissed ye."

"Probably not." Did that mean he regretted it?

"But I did, love. And I'd do it all over again, given half the chance." He glanced in her direction before turning his eyes back to the road.

She wanted to groan, torn between throwing herself at him and doing the sensible thing. "I'm no good with this sort of thing, Angus. It always becomes a total mess, with someone getting hurt in the end." It was nothing but the truth, even if she wanted nothing more than to throw caution to the wind.

"I'm not Stephen, love. I'll not hurt ye."

"And what if I hurt you? What then? Because at this point, you're the only friend I have, and frankly, I can't afford to lose you." Having traveled as much as she did, she had plenty of acquaintances, but few real friends—especially not after Stephen slept with Jennie, who turned out to be far less of a friend than she'd originally thought.

"Ye won't hurt me. And no matter what, I'm adult enough to not give up on our friendship if things don't work out between us."

"You say that now, but it never works out that way, and trust me when I tell you, I don't have a good track record with this sort of thing. It's not worth it. I won't risk it." Her voice was tight, and had skipped an octave in her panic. Why couldn't he see that it would never work?

But she already knew. If he pushed it, she'd cave, leaving her a quivering heap longing for just one more of those mind-blowing, knee-crumpling lip-locks.

"But what if you're wrong, Rowan? Do you really want to be one of those people who are too scared to take a risk and find true happiness? Or those willing to sacrifice true love for the sake of a friendship that'll eventually feel jilted because those involved are ignoring the obvious. I can tell ye, I don't want that—for either of us."

"Well then, it's a good thing I'm not your true love."

Angus burst out laughing, and threw her another glance. "I hope ye realize that just because ye're not planning on pursuing this, doesn't mean I'm not going to. I might have to work a wee bit harder to change yer mind, but truth is, it won't bother me any, and if that kiss was anything to go by, it could be fun."

"Angus… I don't have time for this sort of thing. I need to find my father, not to mention I've got a ton of work to do before opening my gallery. The last thing I need is you distracting me with kilts and kisses."

"Och, is that all it takes to distract ye? Might have to make the kilt a more permanent part of my wardrobe then."

Just the mention of it had her all hot and bothered once more. She'd never be able to keep him at arm's length if he was wandering about trying to weaken her defenses. "Well then, it's a good thing I'm going to be too busy to notice."

"It's not like we won't have plenty of time in each other's company, since I'm helping ye get yer gallery ready." His smile was filled with a mischief she'd have a hard time resisting.

Best to change the subject before she had him pulling over to the side of the road so she could throw his seat back and pick up where they'd left off. Curse him.

"Actually, I have a favor to ask… do you mind coming with me to Edinburgh? I'm going to head to the university to see if I can track down a bit more information and find my mom's college roommate. I figure she might know something that could lead to my father." She could go alone, but she was growing to depend on Angus for moral support. "I can work around your schedule—and will totally make it up to you, though I know I'll owe you my first-born at the rate I'm going."

"I'd love to join ye, though I still wonder if it's wise to go looking for him. I worry ye'll end up hurt and disappointed, love." He reached out and took her hand, holding it tight.

She knew he only wanted to keep her from being disappointed in a father who'd failed to show up thus far, but as her one friend in the area, she really needed his full support—and it stung to think she might not have it. "I know you worry about me, but I need to do this, Angus—and I will, with or without your help and support."

"Och, love, ye know I'm here for ye, and if ye want to go to Edinburgh, I'd love to join ye. I'm happy to help." There was so much emotion in his voice, it dissolved whatever doubts she'd had of him. "I can pick ye up first thing in the morning, if ye'd like?"

"That would be perfect." And it was. Relief washed over her, and left her breathing easy once more. She was back on track for finding her father, and she had Angus at her side.

"The drive to the university in Edinburgh is a long one, so I'd recommend packing a bag since there's a good chance we'll have to spend the night. But seeing that tomorrow's a Friday, the offices should still be open."

She tried not to think about the trouble she could get into if there was a hotel involved—not to mention that cursed kilt. "What about Astro and work? I don't want to be disrupting your schedule."

"Aye, I've got work. But did I not tell ye? Ye're to be my helper—got a client I'm seeing on our way out of town. Be thankful it's just the one, though he does have an entire herd. As for Astro, I'll leave him with my parents who'll spoil him rotten."

"A herd, huh?" Small price to pay for Angus's company and support.

"Aye. But just think—I'll have all weekend long to make it up to ye."

She let out a nervous laugh as his words sent a rush of need pulsing through her body. "Oh, don't worry, laddie. I'll make sure you do."

Chapter Eight

"Are ye not going to help me then?" Angus grinned as the kyloe wandered over towards Rowan and sent her scampering for the fence.

"No frigging way. They're huge." Safely outside the penned area, she watched him with a teasing glare.

"Och, these are just the wee bairns. See how small their horns are?" The farmer brought him the next head of cattle to be vaccinated. He quickly injected the animal, before dropping the syringe in his bucket, and getting ready for the next one. "Ye should go see the big ones—and take yer camera with ye. Scotland's known for them and they make for a good photo, all shaggy and red. Tourists can ne'er resist them. Ye could make a fortune if ye put them in yer gallery."

"Might as well. And they are awfully cute—from over here." She threw him a smile and then wandered back to the vehicle, returning with camera in hand.

Despite his work, Angus couldn't help but sneak peeks of her as she took pictures of the large shaggy red beasts. Her focus was always so complete—so intense. She had such a passion and fire. It always felt barely contained, as if it might burst free at any moment. Yet he didn't think she realized it, always trying to tame it when it should instead be released.

And wouldn't he love to be the one to help her do just that. That kiss... he hadn't been able to stop thinking of it, of her, of how she felt in his arms, how she tasted, the scent of her filling his head, consuming his very soul. He knew he was well and truly sunk, but he didn't mind. Not when it was Rowan who held his heart.

Yet it was all soured by him not being completely honest with her about her father. It was clear she wouldn't abandon her search, no matter what he said. All he could hope to do is steer her away from heartache and whatever her mother feared enough to take to her grave.

Now if only he could keep it all from coming back to bite him on the arse.

He finished vaccinating and deworming the cattle, happy to be on the last one so they could get back on the road, though what he'd do about her search, he hadn't a clue. They were still hours away from Edinburgh—maybe he could distract her long enough for the school offices to close before they got there. Except he'd hate himself for it, and he didn't think it'd slow her down any. She'd likely just wait until Monday when the offices opened once more.

Wandering back to his Rover, he did his best to push his worries aside and managed a smile as she joined him, camera in hand. "Did ye get any good shots?"

"Definitely. You were so right about the beasties—they make for a great picture." She waited for him to toss his stuff in the back of his car, and then offered him the camera so he could have a look.

"I'm filthy, love. I'll muck it up."

"They've got great character—and no one will be able to resist something so shaggy and red." With her back leaning against him so he could see the photos she'd taken, she paged through them. Not that his mind could focus on anything but the feel of her body against his.

"They're great, love." And when she looked up over her shoulder at him with that smile of hers, he was all too tempted to slip an arm around her waist and pick up where last night's kiss left off, photos and farmer be damned.

Once she moved away from him—since he sure as hell didn't have the strength or willpower to do so—Angus cleaned up and settled matters with the farmer. Before long, they were back on the road and making decent time, though she seemed to say less and less the closer they got to Edinburgh.

He tried to keep conversation light, but it was clear she was preoccupied with thoughts of her da. "Ye're worrying me, love. I don't like to see ye so glum."

"What if we don't find my father? What then?" She let out a weary sigh that tore at his soul. "You know, the worst part is not knowing. Why the hell couldn't my mother tell me who he is? I mean, is he that horrible a person? I just don't get it."

He should say something. It was tearing him up. But what he could say? *'Aye, love. Ye're Ma was scared enough to leave her home, family and friends, never to return, and she didn't want ye to go looking for him, which is why she left no clues to his identity.'* She already had so much uncertainty surrounding her father and he knew it would kill her to also wonder about her mother's fear. All he could do was try to ease her worries and keep her safe.

"Things were different back then with out-of-wedlock pregnancies. It might be nothing more than his family not knowing about ye, and he's not contacted ye because it could be awkward for everyone involved if ye went knocking on their front door."

"Yeah—nothing more than a dirty secret he's hoped will stay away." Years of pain tainted her voice with bitterness and it tore at his soul.

"Och, love, that's not what I meant." He reached over and gave her a hand a squeeze needing some physical contact to try and reassure her—and to reassure himself.

"It's nothing but the truth. Why else hasn't he gotten in touch with me? Bastard. It's not like he doesn't know about me. Someone's been putting money in that account all these years—probably hush money to keep my mother and me out of his life. If he had any interest in me, he would have shown up long before now." She bristled in her seat, her entire body stiff.

He couldn't imagine living with those sorts of feelings and doubts all her life. "Ye don't need him, Rowan. And if he hasn't bothered with ye because of what others might think, then ye're better off without him. He's not worth yer time or effort, love. It's his loss."

"I just want to look him in the eyes. Even if it's only the one time. I want to make sure he sees me, so that if he wants to continue to deny my existence, he'll at least have a face to put with his lie."

The hurt, the frustration, and the bitterness… he'd do anything to take away her pain. Unfortunately, there was only one man who could do that—and according to his Ma, Angus couldn't let Rowan find him. He'd just have to try to do right by her—if only he could figure out what that was.

Angus tried his best to turn her mood around, but Rowan said little more, lost in her thoughts. If they did ever find the bastard, he'd have words with the man for doing this to her—and harsh words at that.

Once at the university, they parked and found their way across the school campus, weaving through the college students who were wrapping up their classes and getting ready for the weekend. The sun was setting, streaking pinks and blues across the evening sky, the air damp and holding onto a bitter chill. Angus wanted to hold her close, wanted to pull her into his arms and comfort her, but she kept her pace brisk and he knew the last thing she'd want is him standing in the way of her one and only goal.

They stood at the counter of the registrar's office and waited for the clerk. "I'm sorry to say, but we don't hold onto the housing records more than five years. And ye don't have a name?"

"Just my mother's—Iona Campbell. She was a nursing student." Rowan looked so tense and on edge, she was all but vibrating.

The clerk punched something into the computer, but then shook his head. "I'm sorry. The files don't go back that far. Ye could talk to the Associate Dean in charge of the nursing program—Mrs. Daile. She'd likely be able to help. Back then they tended to house the majors together, so there's a good chance the roommate was also in nursing and Mrs. Daile would know her. Here's where ye'll find the nursing department."

Rowan took the paper the clerk handed her, and gave him a small smile. "Thanks."

Once outside, she gave Angus a hopeful smile, though hesitation and worry tainted her eyes. "It's worth a shot, right?"

"Aye, love. It can't hurt to speak to the woman. She may even have files dating that far back." He kept any doubt from his voice, knowing she'd pick up on it. She was already fighting to stay positive. He didn't want to add to her uncertainty. "We're one step closer, aye?"

"We are." She threw him a sideways glance, her lips turning up in a hint of a smile, and then took hold of his hand, making his heart trip with hope and possibility. "And with some luck, we'll soon have even more information to go on."

"Aye, love." He brought their linked hands to his lips, still unsure of what to do about her father.

Mrs. Daile listened to Rowan's request with a keen interest. Though she must be in her sixties, she didn't look a day over fifty. "Yes, dear. I remember your mother. One of the better students in the program."

"I doubt you were aware of it, but my mother was pregnant during the last few months before her graduation. I'm trying to find my father, and need to track down her roommate. I think she may have been another nursing student, but I'm afraid I don't have a name—for either of them. Any assistance would be greatly appreciated." Rowan sat perched on the edge of her seat, her back stiff as she waited for an answer under the woman's eagle eye gaze.

"I'm afraid we don't give out student information for reasons of privacy." Mrs. Daile pursed her lips into a frown. "I'm sorry. I do wish I could help, but it's school policy."

"Please. I have to speak to her. She's the only one that can help me figure out what happened back then." Practically out of her seat, Rowan's voice was so raw with emotion, it had Angus second guessing himself once more, his guilt tearing at his insides.

He put an arm around her, and pulled her close, wishing he could take away her pain. "Whist, love. We'll figure it out."

"I really am sorry, but I do hope you understand." Mrs. Daile got to her feet. "Before you go, be sure to have a look at the display cabinet. Your mother and one of her close friends both received an award when they were here. It's just at the end of the hall. You'll pass it on your way out. Be sure to take a look. It shouldn't be missed if ye've come all this way to find out about your mother."

"Thank ye for yer time." Angus tried to steer Rowan out of the room, but she stiffened in his arms, not wanting to move. "Come, love. We'll find her another way."

Rowan nodded, with a final glance over her shoulder at the older woman. Once out in the hall, she collapsed against Angus's side, and he knew if she looked at him, he'd see her green eyes sparkling with tears.

But there was something in the woman's insistence… Ignoring his mother's warning, he pointed down the hall. "Look, love. That must be the cabinet."

"Frankly, I don't care about some stupid award. My mom's roommate was the only hope I had of tracking down my father. The chances of finding him were slim to begin with, but without my mom's roommate, I have no hope at all."

When she continued walking past the cabinet, Angus grabbed her hand and pulled her back. "Just a quick look. Then I promise we can get out of here."

With his arm around her shoulder, and her body pressed against him, he turned her towards the glass display case—and it quickly became apparent what Mrs. Daile was trying to tell them. "Look, love. It's yer ma—and another woman. Imogen Murray."

A strangled sound of hope escaped her. "Do you think that's her then?"

"Aye, love. I do. There was a reason Mrs. Daile was insistent about the cabinet. She couldn't give you any information directly, but clearly, she still wanted to help." Angus brushed a stray curl from her face, his touch lingering on her soft skin.

What the hell was he doing? Was he helping her or trying to hinder? Not even he knew.

Rowan squeezed his hand before letting go. "I need to thank her. I don't think she realizes what she's done for me. I'll be just a minute."

He watched her head towards the office, her red locks bouncing down her back, an ease back in her step. It was damn good to see her happy, especially when so much could still go wrong. He supposed, all he could do is try to keep her happy—and safe.

When she came jogging back down the hallway, it was with a smile on her face. She twined her fingers through his and beamed up at him, his worries forgotten in the sparkle of her eyes. "I'm buying you dinner."

"Are ye?" He bit his bottom lip and took her in as if she alone could sustain him.

When she started to go, he pulled her back to him and wrapped an arm around her waist to hold her close. With her curves pressed against him, her body molding to his, he could barely think straight, his only thoughts of her.

She slowly blinked with a deep breath, and then looked up at him through her thick lashes, her full lips turning up in a teasing smile. "Are you not hungry then?"

"Aye, love, I'm hungry. Of that there's no doubt." By the gods, it took all he had to not devour her then and there. To not pin her against the wall and ravage her until she melted under his touch, until she whimpered with need and screamed out his name, riding a wave of passion. How he mustered the self-control to let her go, he hadn't a clue, though he kept his hand linked with hers, still needing to feel her touch. "Come on, love. I know the perfect place."

After a quick dinner, Angus took Rowan to his favorite pub when in the city, settling them down with a couple of pints. "We can track down Imogen's number later, once we get to the hotel."

"Aren't you the least bit worried about finding a room? We've yet to get a place for the night." Her eyebrows perked in an accusatory fashion, as if this would be an 'I told you so' moment in the near future if all the rooms were booked for the night. She'd wanted to get it out of the way before grabbing dinner, but he'd put it off.

"Och, we'll be fine, love. Worse comes to worse, we can drop the seats in the back of my Rover and snuggle up together." Though he was joking, he'd be happy enough to squeeze his six foot three frame into that cramped space if Rowan was nestled against him.

"I'm not snuggling with you, Angus. Not in the back of your Rover or in a hotel, for that matter." She looked so matter of fact, he had to laugh.

"Well, we don't have to snuggle if ye don't want to, love. I'm sure there are plenty of other things to occupy our time." He knew he shouldn't be teasing her with innuendos, yet he couldn't help himself—not when he couldn't get her out of his head. He was never like this, but he couldn't resist her.

The glint in her eyes and the smile on her lips only encouraged him further. She reached over and slapped his arm. "You are so bad, Angus. I've told you—I'm no good at this sort of thing. Stop. Flirting."

His mouth popped open in mock horror. "Flirting? Me? You're the one that's been doing all the flirting, my dear." He then pursed his lips together and shook his head with a stern look. "And I can tell ye right now, ye'll not get me into yer bed no matter how hard ye try. I'm just not that sort of lad, thank ye verra much."

"I'm ignoring you." Yet she laughed and leaned into him.

"So ye are." Seeing her smile return eased the tension knotted in his gut. Things had been emotional for her the last few days, and with such uncertainty still looming ahead, he was happy for these moments to fortify them. Tilting his head towards her empty glass, he slid off the stool where they were sitting by a far counter. "Will ye have another?"

"Sure. We're walking distance to wherever it is we'll be staying, right?"

"Och, aye. There are plenty of hotels in the neighborhood. Back in a sec."

Now that the offices had let out, the bar was crowded with locals as well as tourists from around the world. Being a Friday night didn't help much either. Another pint, and then he'd see about finding them rooms.

He wrestled his way to the bar, and after finally getting the barkeep's attention, made his way back to Rowan, drinks in hand—only to have his back go up when he found a couple of young louts annoying her with unwanted attentions.

CHAPTER
Nine

"LIKE I SAID, the seat's taken. And I'll say it again, in case you missed it the few first times, I have no interest in you guys showing me around. Thanks." Rowan was getting annoyed. Minutes after Angus had gone, two American tourists had come over to ask if the seat was available. Once they'd identified her as a fellow countryman, they'd refused to leave, wanting to show her all the pubs they'd already discovered in the few days they'd been in the city—several of them in the last few hours if their levels of inebriation were anything to go by.

"I promise to show you a good time." He leaned towards her, but when Rowan shifted away it was to find herself coming up against his friend.

She'd come across jerks like this before when she'd been traveling. It seemed every country and every city had its share of obnoxious drunks, and walking away never worked—they only followed and escalated it.

"You guys need to back up. I'm in no mood and you're starting to piss me off."

The guy in front of her tugged on one of her curls so that it bounced when he let it go. "But this is fun. Don't you think this is fun, Jerry?"

Before Jerry could answer, Angus stepped to her side. "Is there a problem? Looks like the lady wants a bit of space, and I want my seat back."

The guys were big, but Angus stood a good six inches taller—and since Angus wrestled cattle and sheep most days of the week, Rowan was sure he also had a bit of power packed into those muscles.

"We were just talking." Jerry looked cocky and stupid, and neither of them was leaving.

Angus shouldered the first guy out of the way so he could move towards his seat and put their drinks down, though he made sure to keep an eye on them at all times. "Conversation's over. I suggest ye take yerselves off to sober up some place."

"Why don't you mind your own business?" The guy pushed Angus with a rough hand to his shoulder.

Angus shifted to shield Rowan, his body coiled tight. She wanted to tell him it was fine if they left—that it wasn't worth the trouble, yet she knew any attempt to walk away would likely result in one of those jerks doing something stupid when they had their backs turned. When the guy tried another push, Angus grabbed the guy's hand, lightning quick, and bent it in an awkwardly painful position, the man crumpling in pain.

Angus applied a bit more pressure, and the guy stifled a squeak, throwing the friend a quick warning to not get involved. "I said it's time you go. Wouldn't ye agree?"

When the guy nodded, Angus pushed him towards his friend. "I suggest showing the lady some respect next time."

Once they'd scurried off with a few hateful glares, Angus ran his hands down her arms, his touch comforting. "Are ye all right, love?"

"Yeah. Just glad you showed up when you did." She tried to keep the tension from her voice, but now that those jerks were gone, her façade slipped lose and she realized just how uneasy they'd made her.

Angus pulled her into the safety of his arms and held her to him, his body still stiff and bristling from the incident. With her head against his chest, she slipped her arms around his waist, the solid feel of him reassuring, and his scent of wool and leather comforting. He kissed the top of her head and then leaned his cheek there. "Ye're safe, love. I promise. I won't let ye come to harm."

And it really was that simple. She knew she could trust him. Not only to keep her safe, but to be there for her—in a way no other man ever had. Not Stephen, and certainly not her father.

Yet she still feared she'd muck it all up if she let it get serious. But maybe, just maybe… Would he be willing to keep things casual until she could get her life sorted out? That way, no one would get hurt if things didn't work out. Really, she shouldn't even go down that road, but she found herself thinking of him more and more with each passing day, and as of late, she didn't think either of them could stay away from each other, even if they tried.

When she looked up at him, her stomach fluttered and her pulse skipped a beat, so she felt like a teenager with a schoolgirl crush. Going up onto her tippy toes, she kissed his cheek. "You're the sweetest guy I know, Angus. No one even comes close."

There was a delicious tension between them and he looked at her with such intensity, she nearly gasped, their kiss in his mother's kitchen still fresh on her mind. His hands trailed up her back, cupping her face as his gaze fell to her lips for a moment before returning to her eyes.

And then he kissed her, slow and sweet, yet with an intensity and passion held in check, coiled tight just below the surface. She lost herself in him as he deepened their kiss, her head spinning as she wished it'd never end. Oblivious to the crowded bar around them, she held onto him, trying to pull him even closer. She couldn't ever remember wanting anyone more.

He pulled away, the air between them charged like a thunderstorm on a scorching summer night. He bit her lip, once, twice and then nuzzled her as he held her to him. His words were but a whisper in her ear, laced with humor and need. "Sweet, huh? Who knew?"

Rowan sat cross-legged in the middle of Angus's bed, the adjoining door to her hotel room open. With her laptop on the bed and Angus sitting behind her, she tapped away, looking for any information on her mom's roommate. "I'm not even sure that's her. There's so little to start with, and it's all unlisted."

"There's also a good chance she got married, and we're looking for her under her maiden name."

He was right. Damn it. "This is impossible." They'd been at it for hours.

"Take a break, love. Ye're getting frustrated." He put a hand on her shoulder and gave it a squeeze. "Bloody hell. Yer shoulders are in knots."

He sat up, and with both hands on her shoulders, started to massage her stiffened muscles, working his way down her back. And damn if the man didn't leave her melting into a puddle of mind blowing amazement. "Oh, god. Don't stop. And how the hell are you still single? Seriously?"

"I don't know, love. You tell me." He laughed, his breath warm against her ear, sending a shiver of want through to her core. "Somehow, ye've managed to resist my charms with little difficulty."

"Yeah, right. Little difficulty." She thought of how he made her knees go weak with each kiss, and if it hadn't been for the lack of privacy in the pub, she'd have jumped him then and there without a second thought. "Your hands are like magic."

"Is that so?" He continued to work the knots out of her shoulders, his fingers strong as they pressed and kneaded, leaving her like jelly. "I'll admit, I don't often do this—at least not on humans."

She looked over her shoulder at him. "What do you mean?"

"I took a course on therapeutic veterinary massage. Usually, I work on horses, but the same principles apply."

"*Horses?*" A smile sprung to her lips, finding it all too funny. "Either way, you're damn good." With a sigh of contentment, she leaned back against him, needing to feel more than just his touch. He wrapped an arm across her chest and snuggled her close.

"It's one of my many hidden talents. Just don't tell anyone, or I'll have all the old biddy's lining up outside my surgery, looking to have their trotters rubbed."

She burst out laughing. "You're so bad, Angus. So very, very bad."

"Aye. Rotten to the core." He nipped at her ear.

Though her body thrummed with need, she couldn't fully enjoy herself when her mind kept straying back to finding her mom's roommate. Hopefully, Angus wouldn't hate her for what she was about to ask.

"Angus… you said Conall was good with computers. Do you think he could help me track down Imogen?"

He let out a deep sigh, and loosened his hold on her as she turned to face him. "I don't know, love. It'd depend on whether or not there's information out there to be found, and more importantly, if he's willing to help ye. He's a cantankerous sort—and that's when he's in a good mood."

"But if the information did exist, he'd be able to find it, right?"

Angus ran a brisk hand through his hair with another weary sigh, as he clearly mulled things over in his head. "Aye. He'd be able to help. Truth is he's more of a legal hacker—testing the security of corporations. If there's something out there, then he'd be capable of finding it—*if* he wanted to help ye."

She smiled. "Leave that to me."

He groaned in mock protest, as a crooked smile crept to his lips. "That's what I'm afraid of, love."

Yet he had nothing to worry about. Not the way he looked at her, the way he made her feel… it was as if she was the only one who mattered, as if anything was possible. "You're amazing, Angus. You know that, right?"

She could resist him no longer. Slipping her hands around his neck, she leaned forward and kissed him, her breath mingling with his, their pulses beating as one. She lost herself in him as their kiss deepened, his hands slipping to her waist to pull her close, his muscles hard against the curves of her body. Her breath hitched as she lost herself in him, her body thrumming with the want of him.

When he slowed their kiss and pulled away, the look on his face sent her stomach plummeting.

"Rowan…" He brushed her cheek with his thumb, her face cupped in his hand. "What are we doing, love? Not that I'm complaining, mind ye. But…"

The way they were going, she knew it'd only be a matter of time before they'd be having this discussion. "I don't know. But do we have to analyze it and put a name on it? I *really* like you, Angus. Isn't that enough?"

"Is it?" He brushed a curl from her face, his touch hot against her skin. "I don't know what ye're looking for, love, but ye've said ye don't want anything serious, and I'm afraid I've ne'er been the kind for a one-night stand."

Damn it. She liked him—a lot. "I wish I was ready for something more, because you're as perfect as they come. But I don't think I can manage anything serious right now." She cupped his cheek and gave him a lingering kiss. "Couldn't we just take it a day at a time? It's just that I need to find my father, I've got the gallery to open, and to be honest, I'm still feeling burned after Stephen."

"Aye, love, I know ye have a lot going on, but truth is I don't tend to be very laid back with this sort of thing." He gave her a shy smile. "I'm sure ye know by now how I feel about ye."

A smile sprung to her lips as she thought of those kisses, his flirting, how protective he was of her, and how he did everything he could to help her. None of it was done lackadaisically or halfhearted, but rather with his full enthusiasm and attention. "Yeah, I sort of noticed, and to be honest, I wouldn't have it any other way. Except…"

"I know, lass. It's just a bit too much for ye at the moment."

"Angus… I don't want to give up what we have between us." She thought of his kisses, how he touched her, and how much she wanted him, thought of what it would be like to have that sort of intensity and dedication when sharing someone's bed. "Are you sure you can't do casual?"

"I've ne'er tried." He looked lost in thought, as if thinking things through. "Honestly? I think we could call it casual, but in the end I'd still fall head over heels for ye. And what then, love?"

She was tempted to take a chance, but the thought of hurting Angus if the relationship got to be too much for her, had her taking a step back. "Forget I said anything. It was a bad idea. Probably best if I go."

When she got to her feet, he took her hand. "Och, love, will ye not stay a bit longer? It's still relatively early, and I could do with the company. Maybe we could just take things slow. Ye ne'er know—we might find yer father and get yer gallery done in no time at all, and then we'd have no reason to stay apart—unless ye found ye wanted to. But this way, it'd give me time to court ye as ye make up yer mind, without things going too far."

"Slow? Not casual?" She supposed there was a difference.

"Aye, love. Slow." Angus brushed his thumb across her lips, his eyes locked on hers. "We'd take our time—get to know each other better. 'Cause I can't do casual. I can't fall into bed with ye and then pretend it was no more important than having a pint at the pub."

She pursed her lips to keep from laughing, while mulling things over. It might work. That way, things wouldn't get very far and if they fell apart, there'd be a better chance of their friendship surviving. "I'm willing to give it a try, though you might need to take the lead on this one. I'm afraid I've never really done *slow* before."

"I like taking the lead." He twined his fingers with hers and brought her hand to his lips.

There was just one thing she needed to know—and she always felt awkward asking. "Just so we're both clear, what does this mean with regards to dating other people? I'm fine either way, but nothing ruins things faster than that sort of misunderstanding, and after Stephen, I don't want any surprises."

His thumb ran lazy circles on the back of her hand. "I'm not terribly good with sharing, but I also want ye to be happy. So we'll keep it to just the two us, but if ye find that ye'd like to date another, I'd appreciate ye telling me in advance—and I'll do the same."

What was good for the goose… "I can live with that."

"Then we should seal it with a kiss, aye?" Cupping her cheek, his eyes softened and he leaned in to kiss her in a slow and most thorough manner. Just as she deepened their kiss, he pulled back, his fingers knotted in her hair and his breath heavy. "We're taking it slow, love. That's what we agreed on, no?"

That kiss left her with a pulsing need that had quickly moved south. Taking things slow would all but kill her. "We did, it's just that I don't know how good I'm going to be at this. I'm not terribly patient."

"Then I'll need to be patient enough for the two of us."

CHAPTER
Ten

ACK IN DUNMUIR, Angus drove through the village with Rowan at his side, mulling over the most recent turn in their relationship. He knew it'd be hard to keep things moving slowly between them, but it was a challenge he was happy to tackle, and maybe it'd make it easier to keep her out of trouble.

As for taking things slow, it could be fun to leave things teetering on the edge with a controlled passion. By the time she decided whether or not to pursue their relationship on a more serious level, the delicious tension between them would have built to a crescendo.

"I'm glad Conall agreed to help us." Rowan shifted in her seat to face him. "I really appreciate you doing this for me. I know you guys don't exactly get along."

"I'd do anything for ye, love." He just hoped she'd understand if it all went to hell and she found out he was keeping things from her.

"I know. It's why you're such a sweet guy." She leaned forward and kissed his cheek, making his heart skip out of control as he ignored the growing tightness of his jeans.

"Och, don't go letting that get around now. I've got my reputation to consider." Angus gave her a teasing smile, and then pulled his car down Conall's drive, his worries returning. With luck, Conall wouldn't be able to find Imogen—and he hated himself for thinking it, when Rowan was absolutely desperate. What a bloody mess.

Parking next to Conall's silver Audi, Angus pushed his worries aside and steeled himself to be civil. "Are ye ready?"

She beamed at him, making him feel even more guilty that he was being dishonest with her. "Never been more ready in all my life. We're one step closer."

She leaned over and kissed him quickly before they stepped out into the brisk air coming in off the sea. With his hand at the small of her back, they walked to Conall's front door and the high-pitched howling yip of a dog. They knocked, but the dog's barking must have alerted Conall to their arrival, since he pulled the door open mere seconds later.

"Come in, then." Conall stepped to the side, holding onto a hyper dog by the collar so it wouldn't escape. As soon as the door was closed behind them, he let go of the wiggling ball of fur. "That's Piper."

Angus reached down to pet the dog, his vet's mind immediately taking in all the details as his hands ran over her body, the dog calming under his touch. Healthy coat and weight. Young—not more than a year and a half. When he stood and the hyperness returned, Angus shushed her with a sharp sound and quick motion of his hand, happy to see her calm down.

"Bloody hell. I've been trying to mellow that mutt for months now. Won't ask how ye did it, but know that I'm damned impressed—and that doesn't happen often." Conall shook his head and continued towards the sitting room.

Rowan smiled up at Angus, but didn't say anything as they followed along. To Conall, she said, "I appreciate the help."

"No worries. Happy to do it." Conall sat down on the sofa and grabbed his laptop off the end table while giving her a lingering smile which had Angus pursing his lips in annoyance. "Who are we looking for?"

"It's my mother's college roommate." Rowan handed him a paper, her neat graphic print detailing the little she knew about Imogen Murray. "It's not much info to go on, but I'm hoping you can still find her."

"Aye. We'll see." Already, his fingers were flying over the keys. His brow furrowed as he continued tapping away, and when he spoke, he didn't bother looking up. "Spirits are there in the cabinet, and ye can help yerselves to whatever's in the kitchen."

Angus didn't say anything about their host, but threw Rowan a look with raised eyebrows. When he took her hand to lead her into the kitchen, he saw Conall's eyes flick to their linked hands before falling back to his search. Even if it hadn't been Angus's intention and it was far more feral and territorial than his normal attitude, he was happy to mark Rowan as his in front of a potential rival.

The kitchen was large and nicely redone, though a bit modern in style for Angus's tastes, with sleek dark cabinets, grey quartz counters and contemporary stainless fittings. Not surprising, Piper followed them, her tail whipping around her skinny body. They found a few cans of soda in the fridge, and didn't bother looking around for glasses. Rowan gave him a smile, but like him, she seemed a bit on edge.

She had a lot riding on what Conall found—while he hoped they came up empty. If he could just figure out whether there was anything to be worried about, he'd then know if he should be helping her find her father or hindering her search.

He pulled her to him, nestling her under his chin, as she slipped her arms around his waist. He breathed deep, her scent of wood fires and peonies filling his head and sending his pulse racing. "It'll be all right, love. Dinnae fash yerself."

She shook her head. "What if he can't find her? I'll have few other options for figuring out who my father is."

How the hell was he supposed to keep her from looking for him without ruining things between them? "Och, love. We'll manage."

She pulled back and looked at him her brow furrowed. "You mentioned my mother was engaged to Conall's dad. Do you think he might know something?"

Angus shrugged, wondering once again how he'd keep her from finding her father. "He was yer mother's betrothed. I don't know how much information she would have given him under the circumstances." Truth was, Iona may very well have told her fiancé about Rowan's father, and he may also know why Rowan's mother left Scotland so scared. Angus might have to pay him a visit—alone. Just until he had more information to go on.

She let out a weary sigh, her shoulders sagging. "Yeah... I guess she may not have gone into any detail, given that she'd cheated on him."

He wanted to groan. He hated to see her looking so defeated. "Maybe Conall will find something. Ye can't lose hope, love."

She nodded and then leaned her head against his chest, quiet for a while. "I'm glad I have you here with me, Angus. With my life being such a mess, taking things slow might actually work."

"Well, I'm glad to hear it." He kissed her, only to have Conall interrupt from the other room, his voice carrying through the home.

"I think I found something."

Angus managed to give her a smile as they rejoined Conall, even though his heart sank with worry.

"I found it awfully odd that there's so little information to be found on Imogen Murray—especially since it's not a terribly common name. There are a few others of course, but not much on this one here. A little more digging revealed why. Are ye familiar with Highland Atlantic Enterprises?"

Angus nodded, and Rowan looked to him for answers. "They're huge around here and have their fingers in just about everything. Made most of their money in oil drilling off the coast."

"Aye, that'd be them. Well, Imogen Murray is the daughter of HAE's founder—and mind ye, it's still a privately held firm. Big money—and that's exactly why ye weren't able to find anything. They keep themselves and their business out of the news, and their information and lives confidential. Her father, Fergus Murray, has quite the reputation for being a ruthless businessman."

"So... does this mean you weren't able to find her?" Worry tainted Rowan's voice, her entire body stiff.

"I didn't say that, did I?" A smirk sprung to Conall's lips as a printer came to life in the far corner of the room. "Here's her information. Name, address, phone, as well as some basic details on the rest of the family. Wasn't sure what ye needed, so figured it'd be best to have more information than not enough."

Conall went over to his printer and grabbed the pages, straightened them with a quick tap and then stapled them. "Here ye go."

Rowan took the papers, her voice unsteady with emotion. "I can't thank you enough, Conall. I totally owe you for this."

"Glad to help." Conall gave her a smile. "And don't think I won't call on ye for payment when I need a dog sitter."

She beamed at him, papers in hand. "You know where to find me."

Angus had to bite back his jealousy at seeing Conall give her the hope she so desperately needed, when all he could do is stand in her way. What the hell was he doing? He was playing a dangerous game, and if it went wrong, he knew he'd lose her. Yet he had to keep her safe. He'd never forgive himself if something happened to her.

They bid Conall thanks and farewell, and hopped in the car to head to Rowan's. She vibrated with excitement, leaving him to force a smile to his lips, his insides torn. Why the bloody hell did his mother give him such a task? Didn't she realize the position she'd be putting him in? And yet he knew, she'd not have asked if she hadn't been truly concerned.

He pulled down her drive just moments later, his smile more genuine this time around. "Shall I see ye in?"

"I'd love that." The way her eyes sparkled with mischief and she bit her bottom lip erased his worries and made him think of trouble he'd be happy to get in.

Angus grabbed her bag from the back of his car and followed her inside. She picked the mail that had been fed through the mail slot in the door and then dropped her camera and bag in the living room, quickly flicking through the envelopes in her hand as she wandered towards the kitchen.

"*Yes.*" She tore the envelope open and pulled out the letter, quickly reading it, a smile jumping to her lips. "I'm officially a gallery owner. The agent was able to rush all the paperwork through."

He swept her off her feet in a hug and spun her around, loving the way she laughed. "Congrats, love. Now ye can get started on fixing it up."

At least dealing with the locals would be a hell of a lot easier than keeping her from finding her father and deceiving her.

"I think this calls for a celebration." Rowan slipped her arms around his neck, and pulled him in close, all her excitement pouring into a deep kiss.

By the gods, he wanted her something fierce. She smelled of sultry wood fires, and with her lush curves pressed against him, it was all he could do to keep control. But this was part of the game he enjoyed playing, and like he'd told her, he was a patient man.

Taking control, he slipped his hands into her hair, and slowly pulled her away just enough to shift his kisses down her neck before nipping at her ear. "Slow, love. Remember."

"Screw slow." Her mouth found his again as she ran her hands down his chest and to his hips, pulling him close.

Lightheaded with need, he mustered all the strength he could to resist her. He took control of the matter by spinning her around in his arms, so her back nestled against his chest, his arm pinning her to him. With his lips at her ear, he teased her, nipping as he spoke. "That's not what we agreed to, love."

She squirmed that luscious arse up against him in frustration, driving him mad. But when she tried to spin back around, he tightened his hold, once more slipping his fingers into hair. Gently, he pulled her head to the side, and unable to resist, nipped and kissed his way up the length of her long neck. Her purrs of need had his jeans going tight. He took several deep breaths to steady himself and then did his best to set the pace, lest he chuck it all and take her there on the kitchen table. Once she softened in his arms, he turned her enough to kiss her, gentle and sweet, making sure to set the pace.

Her arms went around his neck as she nipped at his lips, nuzzling him. "Are you sure?"

His hands drifted to the small of her back as he breathed deep to take in her scent. "Ye know I want ye, but this is for the best. We've got all the time in the world, love. And when I have ye—in a most thorough and complete manner—it'll be because ye're ready for something serious. Until then..."

She sighed. "We'll take it slow."

"Besides, we have more important matters to take care, like getting yer gallery set up."

"And don't forget about finding Imogen." She dug out the papers Conall had given her, as they sat down at the table. "It says she's in East Stratshire. Is that close by?"

"That's not too far from Glasgow. It'd be about a two, two and a half hour drive." Angus checked his watch, relieved it was too late to go out, though he had his doubts he'd be able to keep her from going come morning. "It's already evening, love. No point in attempting it tonight."

"Tomorrow then? If they're as private a family as Conall suggests, it might be easier to just show up, versus calling, which would give them the chance to avoid us."

"Aye, I suppose we could. In the meantime, why don't we go have a look at yer gallery? Ye can start planning things out, and make a list of the things ye'll need. That way when we're going through Glasgow tomorrow, we can pick up some supplies." There'd definitely be a larger selection in Glasgow than locally, and it'd speed things up if they didn't have to place orders. The sooner he could get her distracted with working on the gallery, the better off he'd be.

"Just give me a minute to grab a few things." Rowan returned with a bag slung over her shoulder, and then grabbed her camera. "Ready."

There were clouds starting to come in by the time Angus parked in town, and the strong smell of the ocean rolled in as the tides changed, pungent yet familiar. "Once we're done, I'm treating ye to dinner."

Linking his hand with hers, they walked towards the gallery. The streets were relatively busy with people heading out to grab a bite or wrapping up their days. Angus nodded in greeting to most of the people they passed, and it quickly became clear that most were wondering about Rowan. He was seldom seen wandering about hand in hand with another—let alone with Iona Campbell's daughter. The rumors would be flying.

Truth was he didn't care about the rumor mill—as long as it didn't cause Rowan problems. He was still worried about the reception she was getting from the locals, and didn't know if their relationship would make it better or worse. They would, however, have him to deal with if they treated her wrong—not that she'd likely tell him.

She unlocked the door to the storefront which would soon house her gallery. It really would be a lovely space once they got it fixed up. Whatever she dreamed up, he was sure it'd look amazing.

Angus took measurements of the area while Rowan made up some sketches and took photos. Though they said little, they seemed to find a rhythm, doing their own thing but consulting with each other when need be.

Finishing up his measurements, Angus propped himself up against the desk she was using to sketch things. He looked over at her work, impressed not only with the sketch itself but the design she was planning. "That'll look incredible when it's done, and really shouldn't be that difficult to accomplish. I can't imagine it taking more than a few weeks."

"I really can't wait to get this place open. I'll have to order the art supplies for the classes, but I'll be ecstatic if I can get the gallery finished."

She swiveled in her chair, a smile on her lips as she slipped her arms around his waist. "This might call for a celebration."

"A celebration, is it?" The mischievous glint in her eye told him exactly what she had in mind. "Ye're such a troublemaker."

She got to her feet and nestled herself between his stretched out legs, her body brushing up against his. "Me? *Never.*" Leaning against him, she nuzzled him, her breath hot against his skin when she spoke, tickling his ear and making his pulse race. She left him dizzy and desperate for her. "You on the other hand are nothing *but* trouble."

"I might have to prove ye right—but not today, love. Ye can keep trying, but like I said, I'm happy to set the pace and be patient enough for the two of us." Even if it killed him. By the gods he'd need looser pants if they kept this up much longer.

She pursed her lips. "You're no fun. You know that?"

"Och, now I wouldn't go passing a judgment like that just yet." He nipped at her ear, making her shiver and squirm against him.

"Tease."

"Now that, I won't deny."

CHAPTER Eleven

ROWAN TOOK A deep breath to try and calm her nerves as Angus parked the car, and they walked up the steps to the front door of Imogen's small manor house. They had found the gates at the driveway's entrance pushed open and overgrown with vines, as if they were seldom used. A lucky break, since she didn't want to have to convince Imogen to let a stranger in over some intercom.

Now that she was finally going to meet her mother's roommate, uncertainty had her completely on edge. As if sensing her unease, Angus gave her hand a squeeze. It was easier knowing he'd be at her side, and no matter what, he had her back.

Rowan hadn't even knocked when she heard shouting and the door was yanked open. Not paying attention, the man shouting over his shoulder plowed into her. He grabbed her arms to keep them from going down the stairs in a tangle of limbs as Angus shot a hand out for additional support.

The man took Rowan in as if searching for injuries, his eyes locked on hers. "My apologies. I hadn't expected anyone to be at the door." Realizing he was still holding onto her, he slowly let her go, his face pale and his brow furrowed.

A woman appeared fast on the man's heels, her cheeks red with anger and curses on her lips—only to find unexpected intruders. Rowan felt horrible. It was bad enough they were showing up unannounced, but to stumble on an argument only made the matter worse.

The man shot the woman a final look with a shake of his head as he continued down the stairs. "This is far from over, Imogen. Keep it up and ye'll be hearing from my lawyers."

Imogen watched the man go before turning a steely gaze on the intruders. "Yes?"

So much for first impressions. Rowan would have turned and run if she was there for any reason other than finding her father. "I'm sorry for interrupting your day, but I need to speak with you. Are you Imogen Murray?"

The woman looked at her in question, her eyes narrowing as she took Rowan in. "It's now Imogen Reid. Murray was my maiden name. And you are?"

Rowan took a deep breath and ignored the racing of her heart. "Rowan Campbell and Angus Macleod. I'm Iona Campbell's daughter. I believe you were roommates in college. I was wondering if I could speak to you."

Imogen managed a smile, though she'd clearly been caught off guard. "Of course. Come in." Rowan couldn't help but notice how slight Imogen's Scottish lilt was—as if she'd spent many a year abroad, or had put in the effort to wrangle it into submission.

They were escorted to the living room, and once seated, Rowan took several more deep breaths to try and calm her nerves. She looked at Imogen, easily seeing the young woman who'd been standing next to her mother in the photo.

Imogen gave her a kind smile. "How is your mother? I hope she is well."

Angus gave Rowan's hand a squeeze as she tried to keep the emotion from her voice. "She passed away a year ago."

Imogen's hand went to her lips. "Oh. I'm so sorry, dear. She was a lovely woman and will be missed."

"Thank you." Rowan tried to muster her courage to discuss the reason she came, but needed a moment more.

"You're the spitting image of her, you know. And just as beautiful." Imogen looked at Rowan as if searching her memory for glimpses of the past. "So, how can I be of help?"

"I know this is hardly the conversation to have when you first meet someone, but I hope you'll understand. I'm looking for my father. I don't know who he is, but if you were my mother's friend and roommate, I'm hoping you know who she was dating when she became pregnant." Rowan tried to calm her fraying nerves, but so much hinged on Imogen and what she knew or remembered. Every muscle in her body was taut with tension as she waited for an answer, her heart thrashing against her ribcage.

"I remember she was engaged to a nice lad from her home town, but if she was seeing someone else, I wasn't aware of it, I'm afraid." Her eyes darted from Rowan to Angus in apology. "I will say, there were always lads lingering about with the hope of catching her attention. She was so pretty and such a sweet girl... more than one man had fallen for her charms, despite her betrothal."

"Is there anyone you can remember? Any name at all? Something she said that might give us a clue to his identity?" Desperation had her blinking back tears.

"I'm so sorry. I wish I could be of more help. I'll continue to give it some thought. Perhaps something will come to me."

They stayed a bit longer, but with disappointment weighing heavy on Rowan's heart, she didn't want to linger. Making sure Imogen had all her information in case she remembered anything, they said their farewells.

Angus held her close with an arm around her shoulder as they headed for his car. "We'll find a way, love. Dinnae fash yerself."

She squeezed her eyes shut in an effort to keep the tears at bay, her heart aching. "What if we don't?"

"Whist, love. We'll figure something out." He kissed the top her head and then got her in the car, before slipping behind the wheel and setting off.

She told herself he was right—they'd find another way to track her father down. It wasn't like her to give up, even if the odds were against her. And yet she still found herself swiping at her tears. "I hate this."

"Och, love. Don't go being hard on yerself. Ye've got a new life ahead of ye, and it'll be fantastic whether it's with or without yer father."

"But that's just it. I don't feel like I can move on with my new life until I get this sorted. It's the reason I came, Angus." Didn't he get that? Though why should he when he had his entire family cozily tucked away at home.

"Then maybe Conall's father can help." He let out a weary sigh, his brow furrowed as he took her hand, giving her a quick glance while keeping his eyes on the road. "I just hate to see ye putting yer life on hold for a bastard who's never cared enough to bother with ye."

"Thanks for that little reminder, since I'd obviously forgotten." Her tears spilled over as she looked out the window at the passing scenery, not wanting Angus to see her cry.

"Rowan… I'm sorry. I shouldn't have said that." He brushed her hair from her shoulder, but she still couldn't look at him.

"It's nothing but the truth. And I don't need him to play daddy or make up for the time he's missed. I just need to know who he is—need to look him in the eyes. Just once. And I need to know why—why he never bothered with me. Then I can walk away. Then I'll have the answers I need to truly live my life. Because until then? I'm just going through the motions." She heard him sigh, but still refused to even glance in his direction. She'd look anywhere but at him.

"Aye, love. I can't imagine what it's like, and I'll not pretend to understand how hard this has been on ye. Whatever ye decide to do, I'm here for ye. But… what if ye're better off not knowing who he is? What if there are other factors we don't know about? I worry about ye, lass."

And that was why she couldn't stay angry at him. She knew he only wanted to protect her from getting hurt, yet he didn't know what it was like to live with that sort of question and uncertainty constantly niggling at the back of your thoughts.

She gave his hand a squeeze. "I appreciate that you care enough to worry about me, and you've been indispensable. But I need this Angus— and I'd prefer to do it with you at my side. If you don't think you can support me in this search, then you need to tell me now."

He was silent for what felt like a lifetime, as if debating things in his head, and it made her want to scream that there was clearly only one choice. Couldn't he see that? Yet she bit her tongue and waited, trying not to feel hurt, her tears threatening once more the longer he took to answer her.

He finally gave her the answer she'd been hoping for, leaving her with the one person's support that mattered. "Aye, love. I'll help ye any way I can."

Relief washed over her, as tears escaped to roll down her cheeks. He looked over at her and shook his head, pulling her to his side with a comforting arm around her shoulder, dividing his attention between her and road. "Whist, love. It'll be all right."

By the time they finished shopping for supplies and got back to Dunmuir, night had fallen and she was feeling drained, although a bit more optimistic. They would see about approaching Conall's father, and with luck, Imogen might remember a bit more.

They quickly unloaded the items they'd bought at the gallery, when her stomach started to rumble. She looked over at Angus. He always ate like it was the last meal he'd be getting for months. "You must be starving."

Taking her by the hand, he pulled her close, worry still filling his eyes and creasing his brow. She slipped her arms around his waist, grateful he was at her side, and he enveloped her, closing out the world around them so it was just the two of them. It'd be easy to stay there in the comfort of his arms, but he kissed the top of her head, and then loosened his hold just a little. "Aye, love. Famished. What did ye have in mind?"

"I could attempt to cook." Mentally running down the list of groceries in her cupboards and fridge, she was already wondering how she'd cobble together a meal someone would actually want to consume.

"Ye'll pardon my saying so, but *attempting* dinner doesn't exactly sound like a chance I'm willing to take when I'm starving." Angus tucked a red curl behind her ear, his touch lingering to melt away whatever tension remained between them. "The pub might be easiest—or we could go to the chipper and take home some fish and chips."

"The pub works for me." Quick and easy.

Hand in hand, they walked into the pub and found a booth. Just like when they'd been walking through town, there were more than a few whispers and glances in their direction. She wasn't sure how she felt about it, especially when not all the glances were pleasant. Leaning in to speak to him across the table, she said, "Is it just me or do people seem like they're not too happy about us being together."

Angus gave everyone there a slow stare, as if daring them to keep up their looks to his face. The noise in the pub seemed to dim, his growl low and dangerous. "Pay them no mind, love. Seems they forgot their manners for the day. They're just looking for a bit of gossip."

She thought it might have more to do with one of the town's eligible bachelors hooking up with an outsider—and her mother's past only made matters worse. It bothered her that she was trying to make this place her home, yet it seemed as if she was starting with the deck stacked against her. Normally she'd dig in her heels and let her stubborn streak kick in, making sure they knew she'd be going nowhere, but after the day she'd had, she wasn't sure she had the energy to cope.

Lara strolled up to their table to take their order, a swagger in her step and a smirk tugging at her lips. "Out on a date then? And here I thought our dear Angus might care enough about ye to take ye someplace nice."

More growling from Angus. "Just do yer job, Lara, and take our order."

She glared at him with her head cocked to the side and a hand on her hip before turning to Rowan. "Crankier than a two-year-old without a nap, he is. Don't know how ye put up with it."

After the day she'd had, it was all too much. "You know, I'm really not that hungry. If you could just take me home, I'd appreciate it."

"Stay, love." He grabbed her hand, which resulted in an eye roll from Lara. "Lara was about to apologize and take our order. Weren't ye?"

"Och, aye. My apologies." She glared at Angus, before turning a falsely sweet gaze on Rowan. "So what will it be?"

"Give us a few more minutes to decide. We'll call ye over when we're ready." Angus didn't look away until she turned to go. Once Lara was out of ear shot, he grabbed both her hands in his. "Don't let them get to ye, love."

"It's just been a long day, and not a good one, at that." Crawling under the covers of her bed seemed like just the thing—especially if she didn't have to emerge for a day or two.

"Things will get better, love." Angus leaned in to close the distance between them and cupped her cheek. "Ye've got to believe that."

"And what if they don't? Did I make a mistake in coming here—to Dunmuir? I mean, I came here to look for my father, right? But what's the point if he doesn't want to be found? And it's not like I'm welcome here, thanks to my mom."

Angus's jaw clenched, and when he spoke it was through gritted teeth. "It wasn't a mistake to come here, Rowan. And it's only natural that ye want to find yer father. The only mistake has been made by these eejits who think they've a right to judge others." The last part was spoken louder than necessary. He shook his head. "Come on, love. I'm cooking ye dinner at home."

He grabbed her hand and all but hauled her to her feet. They were out the door before she'd even had a chance to throw her bag over her shoulder. She knew he was angry, but she could barely keep up with the pace he was setting. "You need to slow down, Angus. I'm too short to keep up with you, and though I get that you're angry, you need to take a deep breath and calm the hell down."

She nearly ran into him when he spun on her. His mouth was hard on hers before she even realized what was happening, his arms pinning her to his body. There was no way he was holding back, no taking things slow. Nothing but a primal need and passion, fueled by anger and want. He consumed her, then and there, in the middle of the street, striping her of all other thoughts, until she felt as if her very soul might burn from his kiss.

He then stopped, grabbed her hand and hauled her down the street again. At the first sign that she wasn't keeping up, he scooped her up and threw her over his shoulder, eliciting a string of protests and curses which he proceeded to ignore. He finally put her down when they got to his car. "Get in."

"What the hell, Angus? You don't get to go all caveman on me." Rowan's heart was pounding.

His jaw clenched and he took a deep breath. "Sorry. *Please*, get in the car." Another deep breath, calmer this time. "Please."

She shook her head and got in. At least he was angry on her behalf. Angus didn't say another word while driving, and luckily it was a short ride to his house. Astro greeted them at the door before racing out into the nearby trees.

Rowan followed Angus to the kitchen after dumping her bag and coat by the entry. When he finally turned to her, it was only to get her insides churning. It'd been such a mess of a day, and she could only imagine what the evening would bring. She'd be happy with anything short of a nuclear disaster.

"Do ye want rid of me? I know I've antagonized ye today." His eyes locked on hers, and she could see the lingering lines of anger on his face. But there was more—though what, she didn't know.

Their day and interactions with each other had been less than ideal, but she shook her head no. "I know you mean well, Angus." Closing the distance between them, she slipped her arms around his waist.

He let out a weary sigh and held her close, his cheek pressed against her head as she melted against him. "I swear, love, I can't think straight around ye. Ye leave me dizzy and yearning for ye."

She knew what he meant. Though she kept telling herself she wasn't interested in anything serious, he was the only thing she could think of as of late, and she couldn't ask for a more caring or considerate guy. He was nothing like the man Stephen turned out to be, and she knew she could trust Angus to always have her back. She could count on him— and that wasn't something she'd been able to say about many in her life.

With her heart racing, she realized she'd come to a conclusion. "I don't think I want to take things slow, Angus—or casual."

CHAPTER Twelve

"**A**RE YE SURE, love? I can wait 'til ye're ready." Angus swore every muscle in his body was tense with anticipation as he waited for her answer. He didn't want to rush her into anything, but his heart was aching for her and he wanted her something fierce.

"My mind's made up." She looked up at him with those green eyes and didn't look away, the fire in them one of determination. "I want to give this a shot. Like you said, there's no point in putting my life on hold—and if you're going to catch flack for seeing me, then we may as well do this right."

"Rowan…" By the gods, he didn't think he'd be able to hold back much longer. "Are ye sure this is what ye want?"

A smile tugged at her lips. "I've fallen for you, Angus. Hard." She playfully poked him in the chest. "So you better not go breaking my heart."

"Never." Except that he now felt horrible about keeping things from her.

Worse still was that their visit with Imogen left him bothered. The woman had lied to them. Of that he had no doubt. But he had no clue why. Was she like his mother, trying to keep Rowan from finding her father to protect her? Or was it something else?

"Angus... what is it? You look distracted. I hope you're not already regretting this." Chewing on her bottom lip, she looked away, her smile fading.

Bloody hell, he was a fool. Pushing away any and all thoughts of guilt, he brushed her cheek to get her to look back at him and focused on her alone. Her bright red curls, the porcelain skin and playful freckles, the flecks of gold in her green eyes. "Maybe I need to prove to ye just how happy a man ye've made."

He took a deep breath to try and calm himself, to set a pace that wouldn't scare the poor lass, but with his heart thundering away, and her body pressed against his, there was no hope for it. His fingers tangled in her hair, as her scent filled his head and urged him on, his lips finding hers. With instinct pushing all logical thought from his mind, he devoured her, one kiss after another, as he fisted her hair and pulled her head back so he could move from her lips to the taut length of her pearly neck.

His hand ran over her curves and down to her hips, pulling her close. Little noises escaped her lips as her body melted into his, spurring him on. Without another thought, he had her off her feet and was carrying her to his bedroom, his mouth finding hers once more.

"Dinner..." It was a breathless word spoken against his lips.

"Aye, love." His words were mumbled against her skin and in between kisses. "I'm damn hungry, but dinner just won't do."

Angus glanced over his shoulder to watch her pad across the kitchen towards him, wearing nothing more than the shirt he'd discarded earlier that evening. He'd happily take her again—except that she made him promise to feed her.

She slipped her arms around his waist from behind while he stood by the stove, her hands and cheek hot against his skin. "I think I might start painting the gallery tomorrow. Want to join me? I promise to make it up to you afterwards." She kissed his naked back, and then kissed it again, sending a shiver of need down his spine.

"I wish I could help ye out, love. Ye know there's nothing I'd like more, but I've got patients and a few errands to run." Like going to see Imogen—not that he could tell Rowan of his plans. Especially now that they were officially a couple, he had to try to find out why Iona didn't want Rowan looking for her father, and if Imogen was lying, he needed to know why. He needed to know if Rowan's father was indeed dangerous—he needed to keep her from harm.

"I could come with you, if you like. You know how useful I am around big farm animals."

He put the spatula down and turned to face her, holding her close and giving her a quick kiss. "You should get started on the gallery, love. I can swing by and give ye a hand when I'm done."

As if realizing that he was keeping something from her and being less than honest, her eyes clouded over and she looked away. "I appreciate the help, but I've already eaten up a lot of your time. Don't worry about it. I'll manage."

Now he'd gone and done it. He wanted to groan, his chest tight with the weight of his guilt. He'd never been any good at lying, and now she was misinterpreting it for disinterest.

"Och, love, ye know I'd spend every moment with ye, waking or otherwise, if it were possible. Now, let me get ye yer dinner before I burn it, and decide I'd rather find more productive ways of spending our evening."

With Rowan's loose curls flaming around her face as she slept and the memories of their night together fresh on his mind, Angus had been loath to leave come morning. He'd much rather stay in bed with her tucked by his side so he could take his time waking her in a most thorough manner. Instead he was hours away, getting ready to confront someone about their lies, and grill them on a decades-old event no one wanted to speak of.

"Mr. Macleod?" Imogen looked around for Rowan, and then stepped back. "Come in."

"Please, Angus is fine. I'm sorry to bother ye yet again, but I really need to speak to ye." Angus followed her into the sitting room and took a seat across from her so he could make sure to catch any signs that she may be lying. "It's about Rowan's father. Ye must pardon me for saying so, but I believe ye were less than honest with us the other day. I'd like to know why."

She cocked her head back and her eyes narrowed. "I beg your pardon."

"I'll admit, I'm a horrible liar myself. But I think it's the reason why I'm so good at catching others at it. And truth is, I'm not here to necessarily find Rowan's father, but what I do need to know is why Rowan's mother refused to tell her—even on her deathbed—who her father is."

"And how am I supposed to know? I think you should go." She got to her feet, but he just sat back, stretched out his legs, and locked his eyes with hers.

"Tell me why no one will speak of the man—why no one has a name." Angus saw her eyes flick to the corner, and he knew there was more to it. "So ye do know. Ye know who he is."

"Get out!" Her cheeks turned a mottled red, her jaw clenched.

Angus stood and squared off with her. "Who is he?" He glanced in the direction her gaze had strayed, but couldn't linger long enough to investigate the fireplace mantel with its candles, pictures and porcelain figures. "Tell me. Please. She won't let it rest until she knows who he is."

"Get out, or I'm calling the police." Imogen pointed to the door, her hand shaking.

"Aye, I'm going. But if ye think she's going to stop looking, ye're mistaken. I'm begging ye to reconsider. She deserves to know." Angus headed for the door. "Ye've got our number should ye change yer mind."

Angus left, now sure the woman knew more than she was saying. He pounded the steering wheel. What the hell was everyone hiding? What were they scared of?

He needed more information, and he hated to admit it, but there was only one person he knew who might be able to help. Conall.

It was amazing what one was willing to do for love—and he was hopelessly and truly head over heels. He hadn't wanted to admit it to himself when they had barely been dating, but after last night, there was no denying how he felt about Rowan. He loved her—and he'd do whatever it took to see her happy and whole.

He spent the long drive back to Dunmuir and Conall's place mulling over the growing mystery. He knew his mother didn't have any other information. She wouldn't hold back, trusting him enough to deal with the information accordingly. However, Imogen didn't know him and clearly didn't trust him, but he thought there was more to it than trying to protect Rowan. He just needed to figure out what.

Conall answered the door while attempting to wrangle his pup, his eyes going wide when he saw who his visitor was. "Angus. What's happened?"

"Can I come in?" Angus was itching to get started, but knew it'd be easy to put Conall in a mood. "I need yer help."

Conall nodded and stepped to the side, finally letting the dog loose once the door was closed. He headed for the sitting room, leaving Angus to follow. "Is it Rowan?"

"In a way. I need ye to dig up all ye can on Imogen Murray—beyond the basic information ye gave Rowan."

"Her mother's roommate? Seems like ye're all going to an awful lot of trouble." Conall grabbed his laptop, his fingers a blur as they tapped out their random melody. "Did ye not find her at the address I gave ye?"

"We did, but she's lying to us about something and I need to know what." Angus absentmindedly petted the pup.

"Ye know, if ye tell me what this is really about, there'll be a better chance I'll be able to help ye." Conall gave his head a shake, only looking up for a moment.

Angus let out a sigh, knowing Conall was right and dreading the indelicate matter, given who Conall's da was. "Rowan's looking for her father. She doesn't have any information on the man and was hoping the roommate might help."

Conall sat back, his eyes locked on Angus. "I'd have appreciated knowing that from the start, aye?"

"I know." Angus held Conall's gaze. "Will ye still help?"

He said nothing for a bit, his gaze hard, but then turned back to his laptop. "Ye're lucky I like her—and before ye go getting yer knickers in a twist, I know ye've made yer claim. I'm not like that and that's not the way I meant it."

"Well I appreciate yer honesty—and yer help." Angus sat back, the knots in his shoulders cramping despite the relief that washed over him.

"Let's see what we can find—though ye know we should be speaking to my Da."

"I didn't want to go digging at old wounds." Angus tried not to think of what he'd do if he found out who Rowan's father was. He supposed it depended on who the man was. Yet the thought of keeping it from her, no matter what the reason, had him breaking out in a cold sweat. She'd never forgive him if she found out. "Do ye think he might know?"

Conall shrugged. "Might as well find out." He closed his laptop and stood. "Are ye coming then?"

"Damn right, I am."

Conall called ahead to let him know they were coming, and the tea was already made and set out by the time they got there. Angus shook Gordon Stuart's hand. "Thank ye for taking the time to see me."

"Sit, lad." Gordon folded his tall frame into the chair. "What can I help ye with?"

Angus looked to Conall, knowing it'd be best for him to start the conversation. "Da, ye need not discuss any of it if ye don't want to."

"Is it about Iona's lass? The folks in town mentioned she'd moved into the cottage."

"Aye, Da. She's looking for her father and has had little luck."

The older man nodded. "Doesn't surprise me. Iona refused to speak of the incident." He let out a weary sigh with a slow shake of his head, emotion tightening his voice. "And don't judge Iona—or her daughter—for what happened back then. I knew it wasn't meant to be—a lass like Iona wasn't meant for a simple life in a small town."

"Sir..." Angus hated digging at old wounds, especially when it was clear it still affected the man. He could only imagine how he'd feel if Rowan left him for another, especially if they were engaged to be married and she was carrying another's child. "Did Iona say anything about the man? Anything at all?"

Gordon let out a deep breath and sat back in his seat. "Aye, she did. I insisted on knowing, and given our situation, she had a hard time denying me. Not that she told me his name."

Angus went from hopeful to disappointed in a heartbeat. "What *did* she tell ye?"

"She told me she loved him and he was a good man. That was something at least—that her betrayal was for love." He motioned to Conall, his movements slow and weary. "Get us a drink, son. Tea's not quite strong enough for this sort of conversation."

Conall did as he was bid, while his father continued. "Iona said that she and the child would be well taken care of, but she'd have to leave

Scotland and wouldn't return. When I asked her why, she told me that the father of the child didn't know she was pregnant, and she couldn't let him find out."

Angus sat forward in his chair. "So he doesn't know about Rowan?" Maybe the man wasn't a bastard after all.

Gordon shrugged. "I couldn't tell ye, lad. But at the time, I don't believe he did. I will tell ye that she was scared—though if the father didn't know of the child, then I'm not sure who had her so frightened."

"Was she just upset or truly frightened?" Angus had to know. It would be the difference between being able to tell Rowan of her father or having to keep it a secret.

"Scared like I'd never seen her before—and Iona Campbell wasn't one for theatrics or hysterics. She knew leaving like she had would all but do her father in—and it did—yet she still went."

"And Iona didn't say who had her so scared or why?" Bloody hell. Angus didn't know what he was going to do.

"If the lad didn't know he was to be a father, then I can only imagine it was someone close to him. But she refused to say, worried that she might cause me trouble." Gordon gave his head a slow shake. "I loved the lass—and she was a good person, no matter what ye'll hear others saying. I forgave her long ago and even told her I'd raise the child as my own, but she said she had to leave. Left me heartbroken, I'm afraid."

With his head spinning, Angus thanked Gordon for his time, before heading back to Conall's home. Conall said little during their drive, but his mood had darkened considerably and Angus wondered if he'd still be willing to help find Rowan's father and dig deeper on Imogen.

"I truly appreciate ye taking me to see yer father, Conall. I know it was hard for him."

"What ye don't know is that my father's ne'er been truly happy. My mother was no more than a distraction from his broken heart and though he loved her in his own way, it wasn't enough—and my mother knew it."

Angus knew Conall's parents had divorced when they were still in secondary school. "I can't imagine it, and it's all the more reason I sincerely mean my thanks. I know we've not always gotten along in the past, but I appreciate ye putting our past behind us to help."

Angus let out a sigh. "Let's see what we can do to help the lass, aye? There's no point in having more tragedy come out of this mess."

They sat down in the living room with the laptop, and it didn't take long for Conall to start pulling up information on Imogen. The printer was spitting out pages so fast they were spilling out onto the floor. Conall didn't even look up, but Angus started to gather and reorder the pages.

He looked at several of the pictures. Pictures of Imogen with her husband and children. Another of her and her father at an HEA meeting and yet another of the HEA board of trustees. Angus took a closer look, and recognized the man who had plowed into Rowan the first time they were at Imogen's. Imogen's father also looked familiar.

He turned his attention to the pages of text. Most were about business acquisitions and mergers. Some rumors of new products or speculations about drilling. Rumors of the old man's failing health and more speculation as to what would become of the business. Looked like the son was set to take over.

"Can we dig further back into the past? I don't know that current news will hold many clues as to what happened over twenty-five years ago."

"I'm working on it, but there's not a whole lot online from that time period. Mostly business and real estate transactions, births, deaths and marriages." More paper shot out from the printer.

Angus sighed and ran a rough hand down his face. "I just don't know. Maybe I was mistaken about Imogen. And even if she was lying, who's to say it was about Rowan's father?"

Conall shrugged as he continued to type, not bothering to look up. "What does yer gut tell ye? In my experience, it's seldom wrong."

"It tells me that she's lying about not having any information about Rowan's father." He flipped through the pages again, his mind churning but coming up empty. His gaze landed on the photo of the company heads, which could easily pass as a family photo. "Do me a favor. Search for problems involving Imogen and this bloke here—looks like he's her brother. When we went to visit her the first time around, he was there and they were having a row. Nearly knocked Rowan down the stairs in his anger."

"Well, ye know the old man's in ill health. According to this list, they are indeed siblings. His name's Rory Murray. Could be that with the patriarch no longer able to head up the company, there might be some in-fighting on who'll be taking over." More tapping on the keys. "Aye. Looks like the son wants out. Wasn't ever really much of a businessman, but looks like he married into another powerful business family. Guess there was no chance of escape, though they've divorced since then. Also looks like Imogen has been there as her father's assistant."

"Still doesn't tell us what she was lying about." Angus replayed the short conversations he'd had with the woman and turned up empty.

"I'll keep digging, aye? But now I'm going to kick ye out. I've got work to do."

CHAPTER
Thirteen

ROWAN IGNORED THE stares and whispers, a smile on her lips, as she grabbed a bit of yogurt and fruit at the grocers for a late lunch. After the night she had in Angus's arms, she didn't give a damn what they said. Nothing could ruin her good mood.

"Thank you." She got her change from the woman behind the counter, giving her a big smile and refusing to play their games. This would be her home, and she'd do her best to win them over—if not for her sake, then for Angus. She wouldn't allow it to become an uncomfortable place for him.

"Hmph." A scowl of pursed lips faced her as her groceries got bagged none too gently. "Is Angus not with ye today? Surprised he managed to get free of ye."

She bit back all of the smartass responses bubbling to her lips. *He's actually tied to my bed.* Or maybe… *That's because he's so exhausted after the night we had, that he's lying in bed in a spent heap.* Instead, she refused to rise to the bait. "He's working, but I'll be sure to send him your regards. Have a lovely day."

Ignoring the tightness in her chest, she told herself it would take time—but it *would* happen. She'd win them over one by one. And then maybe the feeling of constantly being watched would go away. She glanced around but didn't see anyone paying her any outward attention, even if it still felt like her every move was being scrutinized.

She wandered back towards her gallery to finish painting. Her good mood had spurred her on during the morning, and she'd gotten plenty done. The electrician would still need to come, but she hoped to have the place open in just a few weeks' time.

Just a bit more to do before heading home, though she swore Angus said he'd be swinging by. Pulling out her cellphone, she checked the time and to see if she'd missed any calls or messages. It was after four, and no one had tried contacting her.

Unlocking the door, she stepped through, and found an envelope that had been pushed through the mail slot. There was nothing written on the envelope, but once she'd unfolded the paper within, she knew the letter was for her.

The pounding of her heart echoed in her ears as anger bubbled up in her chest. Taking a deep breath, she held onto it until her lungs burned and then calmly slipped the nasty note back in its envelope before tossing it in her handbag. She picked up the paint brush and popped the lid on the can of paint, but her focus was shattered and her attempt at work was futile. Even her appetite had vanished.

Knowing she wouldn't get anything more done, she grabbed her few groceries and locked up. More paranoid now that she'd been threatened, she kept a sharp eye on her surroundings and headed to the safety of her car. Once there, she quickly texted Angus to let him know she was no longer at the gallery and was heading home.

She thought about swinging by his house, but if he was still busy with patients, she wouldn't feel comfortable letting herself in and waiting without him there. The stares and whispers were one thing, but this pushed the matter to a whole new level. Now that she'd taken the leap with Angus, she found herself desperately wanting him to hold her and tell her things would be fine.

So, where the hell was he? Up at seven that morning, it's not like she'd slept in. Yet Angus was already gone by the time she awoke, a pot of coffee made. He'd left her a note saying to make herself at home and he'd catch up with her at the gallery later in the day. But the day had come and gone and there was still no sign of him.

Once she'd decided she wanted a serious relationship with Angus, she could have sworn he would be the one guy who wouldn't make her second guess herself—or second guess her decision to sleep with him.

Whenever she'd given in to a night of passion, it seemed she could never quite escape the niggling thought that she'd made a mistake once she was looking at things in the light of day. She'd have bet the house that Angus wouldn't have her doubting herself, and yet... here she was now wondering if he was going to show up or call.

She debated dinner once she got home, but it only made her think of Angus, and whether she should plan something for the two of them, or eat on her own. As if picking up on the annoyed girlfriend vibe she was sending into the universe—since she supposed that was what she now was—her phone rang.

Angus apologized and said he'd be by in a few minutes, and though she was relieved to have finally heard from him, she had to force her doubts and annoyance away. He was a busy man, after all, and it's not like men were known for their good communications skills when it came to relationships. Sure, they could talk a storm around business, sports and politics—but dealing with relationships? Not so much.

True to his word, he was there just minutes later. "Sorry I was late, love." He leaned in and gave her a quick kiss as she stepped to the side to let him in.

She forced a smile to her lips. "No worries. I was just thinking of dinner. Have you eaten?" She looked at him, but only found dark circles under tired eyes, his gaze refusing to settle anywhere for long. What the hell was up?

"Nae, love. And I'm starving. Do ye want to head to town for a bite?" He brushed a stray curl from her face, his touch lingering.

The knot in her gut loosened just a little, and before she could think, she had her arms wrapped around his waist, the feel of him comforting, her anchor in a storm. "I don't want to go back to town. Not tonight."

Something in her voice must have betrayed her, because he pulled away and looked at her, his brow furrowed. "Hey... what's happened?"

She debated whether or not she should tell him about the letter. If she did, he'd worry and heads would likely roll. If she didn't, he'd still worry—and if he found out later on, he'd be furious with her for not being honest with him. In the end, it wasn't a risk she was willing to take. She knew there was no place for dishonesty in a relationship—not if you wanted it to survive.

"Promise me you won't get angry." She dug around in her bag and pulled out the envelope. "Promise me, Angus."

"I'll make no such promise." He snatched it out of her hand, his jaw already clenched as he yanked the paper out. Angus unfolded it and immediately tensed, his voice straining with fury as he read the note. *"You're not welcome here. Leave Scotland, or you'll be sorry you stayed."*

His fist curled around the paper, crushing it, his teeth clenched tight as he spoke. "I'll murder the bastard who sent ye this."

"Forget about it, Angus. It's nothing more than one of the locals venting." She let out a weary sigh, even if it felt good to know she was no longer alone. "It's been a long day and I'd rather not do this. Besides, it's a plain paper, plain envelope, and even the font is typical. Not even the police could manage to figure out who sent it."

"Grab yer things. It's not safe for ye to stay here on yer own." He started to pace the floor, the kitchen far too small to contain him.

"I'm not going to let anyone scare me off." She stepped in his path and looked up at him. "This is why I didn't want to tell you."

"How could ye think of *not* telling me, Rowan?" His eyes roamed over her face, while his hands ran down her arms. "I promised to keep ye safe, and I meant it. Now get yer things or I'll get them for ye—and I'll warn ye now, I haven't always been known for my fashion sense."

"I'm glad I have a choice in the matter." With a glare, Rowan spun around and headed to her room, cursing under her breath as she tried to curb her annoyance. She threw a handful of items in her carry-on bag, including her camera, and headed back downstairs. "I'm only staying for a day or two."

"Ye'll stay until it's safe." He hefted her bag over his shoulder and with a gentle hand on the small of her back, tilted his head at the door.

They drove to his home in silence, his speed way too fast for the narrow lanes, though she supposed he'd been traveling them his entire life. She knew he'd overreact, and it should bother her, but after her past relationships, it was a welcome change, since it meant he cared.

The sound of his tires crunching the gravel of his drive echoed in the car as he pulled in towards his home. With the car in park, he reached out and twined his fingers with hers, bringing her hand to his lips. "Ye'll be safe here, love."

They got out of the car and headed in, though the conversation wasn't over. She appreciated his concern and thought it sweet, but she didn't want him getting paranoid and stringing villagers up by their ankles. "I was safe at home too, Angus. It's nothing more than one of the locals being grumpy that I've snagged one of their cutest bachelors."

He let out a long sigh and pulled her to him, wrapping his arms around her waist as a smile managed to tug at his lips. "*One* of the cutest? And who would the others be, pray tell? I know old crabbit MacDonald could give most men a run for his money, but since I've got all my teeth, I'd think that'd bump me up to a separate category. No? And *cute*? Really? Ye don't want to rethink that? Perhaps *dashingly handsome* would be more appropriate? Or maybe *sexy and gorgeous* would be a better fit?"

He waggled his eyebrows up and down at her until she burst out laughing and the tension in her chest slipped free. She playfully slapped his chest as he pulled her in for a kiss that made her toe curls. "You really are too much, Angus."

"And I'm all yers, love." He spun her around and slapped her bottom. "Dinner. I need something to eat, and if I don't get food soon, I'll find other ways to satiate my hunger."

Angus had dinner on the table in record time, though how he managed such a tasty dish of spaetzle with chicken and mushrooms in a sherry cream sauce, while looking like he was doing nothing more than throwing things into a pan, was beyond her. A salad of spring greens with a balsamic vinaigrette helped to cut the richness of the sauce, as did the dry white wine he served.

Conversation was kept to a minimum as they finished their meal. Though Angus threw the occasional smile in her direction, she also found him lost in his thoughts with his brow furrowed when he didn't think she was looking at him. Was it because of the note? Or something else?

It was too easy for her paranoia and past experiences to get to her, leaving her to wonder if it was about their relationship—and their night together. The logical side of her said he'd been busy and was distracted by the note. Why would he ask her to stay over if he didn't think things were going well? But there was still a niggling worry that something definitely felt off, and it went beyond the note.

She couldn't take the silence much more, but told herself she was being foolish. She tried to ignore the knot forming in her chest, and chewed on her words—repeatedly—until there was no holding them back. "Is everything all right?"

He looked up at her with a smile, but it didn't reach his eyes. No sparkle in that sea of blue, no humor. "Aye, love. Just a bit distracted—and none too happy about that threat."

She tried for humor, hoping it would pull them both out of their funk. "You know, it's probably just one of your many heartbroken girlfriends."

"Damn it, Rowan. This isn't a joking matter." He shook his head and stabbed at his food, not saying another word.

"Well, pardon me." She pushed her chair back and put her plate in the sink, rinsing it off before stacking it in the dishwasher.

"Rowan... I'm sorry, aye? It's just been a long day and I'm worried about ye." He sat back, his eyes locked on hers.

"Well, you don't need to worry about me. I've always managed just fine on my own." Not quite knowing what to do with herself, she started to clear the counter of anything that hadn't been put away while Angus cooked.

"Would ye leave it?" When she walked by, he grabbed her hand and pulled her to him. "Come sit with me, love."

He pulled her into his lap, and she let him, leaning her head against his shoulder as he held her tight. "Tell me you have no regrets, Angus."

"Och, well, there will always be some regrets, love. Like the time I decided to talk back to my Ma and she nearly tore my ear off, or the night at university when Iain and I had just a wee bit too much to drink and ended up at the school stables trying to ride some poor horse bareback when we could barely stand. I nearly broke my arm and Iain threw his back out. Couldn't walk right for weeks. But if ye're asking whether I have any regrets where ye're concerned, the answer is no. I haven't a single regret, love. Not one."

She let out a long sigh, her head against his shoulder as he held her close. "Then why do things suddenly feel awkward between us?"

"It'll pass, aye? Dinnae fash yerself. There's nothing to worry about."

So why did that feel like a lie?

CHAPTER Fourteen

NGUS HAD SPENT the last few weeks waking up with Rowan in his arms, and should be ecstatic. Yet he couldn't enjoy himself, couldn't settle with his conscience eating away at him, especially when she only became more insistent about finding her father. He'd have to tell her soon, though the thought of making a confession like that had his gut in knots.

He'd been lying to her ever since she got to Scotland and his mother pulled him into this mess—and it was killing him. It'd been a month of manipulating things to keep her from searching, to keep her from getting into trouble. The threatening note only made him paranoid, and though there hadn't been another—that he was aware of—he was still worried about her safety.

With a promise to see Rowan later that afternoon, Angus spent the day seeing patients with nothing but his ever-present guilt for company. The more he lied to Rowan and tried to keep the truth from her, the more his mood soured. Even the animals were getting nervous around him.

The threatening note could easily be one of the locals trying to scare Rowan off, but knowing Iona had been frightened when she left Scotland, he had to wonder if this had to do with their search for Rowan's father. Had their questions stirred the hornet's nest? News and rumors traveled fast around these parts. Even news of Rowan's arrival in Dunmuir might be enough.

He wrapped up with his last patient, and then knowing he had a bit of time before meeting up with Rowan, he decided it'd be best if he vented some of his frustrations. Needing some company of the male variety, he headed to his best mate's home.

Iain MacCraigh answered the door, a smile on his face. "Bloody hell. Thought ye forgot the way to our house—it's been weeks. Months." Iain stepped to the side. "What's wrong with ye? Ye look like shite."

Angus pursed his lips and glared at his friend while walking into the ancient home. "And a hello to you too."

Iain followed behind him, clasping his hand on Angus's shoulder. "Ye've got the rumor mill churning, lad."

"I'm sure I do, though I wish they'd all just bugger off and leave it the hell alone." Angus looked around, searching. "Where's yer better half?"

"Coming up right behind ye." Iain tilted his head towards his fiancé, Dr. Catriona Ross.

Angus turned and gave Cat a hug and a kiss on the cheek, his mood lightening for just a moment. "How are ye, my dear?"

She took a step back and looked at him. "Better than you are, by all accounts. Come and have a seat."

They settled in the library by the fire, and it didn't take long for Iain to have a glass of whisky in each of their hands. Angus took a long sip, and savored the smoky taste of the spirits as it filled his head, before slipping down his throat like a molten sun, spreading its warmth. Already, he felt better.

Angus held his glass up. "Thank ye for that."

"Now are ye going to tell me what's going on?" Iain sat back, with Cat nestled against him, his eyes pinned on Angus. "I'll not even start to tell ye the rumors circling, since I know ye've got a wee bit of a temper when it comes to this sort of thing."

"I can imagine, aye? They're talking about Rowan, no? And her mother." His hand tightened around his glass until his knuckles went white, and he was forced to take a deep breath through clenched teeth.

"They're also talking about you and Rowan being a couple—shacked up together, no less. And don't even get me started on the rumors that were circling a few weeks ago. Said ye nearly had her then and there on the street before slinging her over yer shoulder and carrying her off to yer bed. They say ye've barely been seen since." Iain's eyebrow perked in question, a smug smile dancing on his lips. "Any truth to all of that or are ye going to tell me the townsfolk have gone completely mad?"

Angus groaned at the thought that his parents were probably hearing those same exact rumors. But he'd come to talk and vent, so he might as well. "It's not far from the truth."

"Bloody hell, lad. So why the mood then? I'd think ye'd be happy as a pup who found the Christmas goose unguarded." Iain looked like he was trying to contain his laughter, and it didn't go unnoticed by Cat who slapped his chest. He mockingly rubbed the area she'd hit, a teasing smile on his lips. "Watch it, woman. That hurt."

Ignoring their playful banter, Angus sighed, his gaze lost in the liquid gold of whisky, the flames from the fire dancing on the spirits. "Things are a bit strained. All along, she's said she didn't want any sort of serious relationship, and though I've convinced her to give things a try, I worry that she's already regretting it, especially since I'm only mucking things up."

"Angus… I don't want to speak out of turn, but ye're my best friend, so I'm going to open my gob anyway." Iain sat forward, elbows on his knees. "Ye always fall for the ones who aren't interested in settling down. Ye're going to get yer heart broken."

"In the past, it suited me just fine that they weren't looking for anything serious. Neither was I, when I still had to finish with my studies and get my practice started." Angus shook his head, thinking of how Rowan made him feel, his heart swelling at the mere thought of her. "But now…"

"It's different with Rowan." Iain finished his thought for him and linked his hand with Cat's, his eyes on hers with a fierce intensity of love and devotion. "Aye, I know."

Cat gave him a sympathetic look. "Just be yourself, Angus. She won't be able to resist yer charms for long."

"Ye're a kind woman, Cat, and I can only hope ye're right. Unfortunately, there's more." Angus debated how much he should tell them. "Someone's left her a threatening note. Don't know if it's because she's gotten someone's knickers in a twist over opening a gallery in town or if it has to do with more personal stuff. Either way, I'm none too happy and it's only complicating matters further between us."

Iain sat forward and looked at him—really looked at him. "Is that all? 'Cause I'll admit, I feel like there's something else eating at ye. Ye've ne'er been one to deal with a guilty conscience, and you look damn guilty, lad."

Angus groaned, his chest tight and his temper flaring. "Truth is, I'm keeping things from her—things she certainly has a right to know, but that could put her in harm's way since the lass refuses to look before jumping. And it's killing me to not be completely honest with her."

With a shake of his head, Iain gave him *that look*. The one that told him he was being a fool. "It'll bite ye in the arse. Ye know that, aye?"

Frustration bubbled up in his chest, threatening to choke him. "*I know.* But what the hell am I supposed to do? I need to keep her safe—that's my first priority, no?"

"Och, aye. And ye can only hope she'll forgive ye for it."

Angus was in no better a mood when he parked in town. But it didn't matter. He needed to make sure he wasn't adding to Rowan's worries and that meant setting aside his guilt and worries. There was nothing he could do until he had more information to go on and could make sure she'd be safe.

The glass front to the gallery made her easy to spot while she sat at her desk, her attention on her laptop. He tried the door and then knocked, happy to see she locked it, just like they'd discussed soon after the threat. If he could spend each day with her, he would, but he couldn't neglect his patients, and he knew Rowan would pick up on his worries and guilt, impossible to keep the charade up for the entire day.

"Hey, love." Stepping to her side, he swept the hair from her eyes, letting his touch trail down her cheek. Cupping the back of her neck, he pulled her in for a slow kiss, so incredibly happy to see her again. His pulse raced as she melted against him, his head dizzy with need. When he managed to pull himself away, he was breathless. "Did ye have a good day?"

"It's better now that you're here." Her smile had him leaning in to kiss her again as she batted him away with a laugh. "Managed to get the glass cases finished, and your friend came by and started on the electrical. Said he should have it done in the next day or two, since most of the wiring is up to date. All he has left to do is put in the lighting and then run the wires for the kiln."

"Does that mean ye'll be open for business soon?" Perhaps opening the gallery would give the locals a chance to get to know her better—especially if some of them signed up for the classes she'd be offering. And keeping busy with her classes would probably do a better job than he was of distracting her from her search.

"I don't know. I still need to get my pictures printed in various sizes, and then I'll need to put together a list of the classes I'll be offering, but… I think it's going to have to wait. I've spent way too much time on this, when I really should be looking for my father. Even if it seems like a longshot, I haven't given up hope. Someone knows something. I just need to track them down."

"There's plenty of time for that later, love. Why don't ye let it rest a bit while ye get yer life settled here, and then maybe we'll come across some new leads. We don't have a whole lot to go on right now." Damn it. She'd never give up and his attempts to stop her were only putting a wedge between them. Already, his words had her eyes clouding over. "Come, love. Let's go home. It's been a long day, and I have some new recipes I want you to try."

The crease in her brow faded as a smile worked its way to her lips. "Does this mean I'm your culinary guinea pig?"

"Aye, love. Just be thankful my experiments have come a long way from when I first started. My meringue fiasco got me banned from my Ma's kitchen for over a year. It took months before we could turn on the oven without having the house fill with smoke." When she laughed, it eased the knot twisting around his heart.

Luckily, the ride home was a short one, especially since his thoughts kept nagging at him, telling him it would all go wrong. If she finally decided to question Conall's father, it would all go to hell, especially once she found out Angus had already spoken to him about Rowan's mother. He couldn't ask the man to lie on his behalf, and Gordon was the next logical choice if she chose to go looking.

He'd just have to distract her, and he'd start with a meal that would blow her away. If he could make her happy, then maybe she'd concentrate on the things she *did* have in her life, rather than the things that were missing.

Astro was ecstatic to see them, and after a quick jaunt out to mark his territory, he followed them back into the kitchen with a bark of excitement and a full body wiggle. He watched Rowan play with his pup as her laugher filled the room, and knew his home would feel empty without her in it. It'd be impossible to go back to the way it was before she'd come into his life. Unable to resist and needing to feel her touch, he stole a quick kiss.

"Anything I can do to help?" She wandered over to the counter when he started pulling out ingredients.

"Not a thing, though I hope ye're hungry. We're starting with a cheese soufflé." He cranked the oven to a temperature that could handle both the soufflés and the potatoes, quickly mixed the spuds with some olive oil, garlic and rosemary, and then tossed them in the oven.

"Soufflé? Is that all?" She gave her head a shake and her smile widened. "You're always full of surprises."

"I like to keep ye guessing." Angus whipped the egg whites and added the cheese, checked the temperature of the oven and put them in to bake.

"So what else is on the menu?" She slipped her arms around his waist from behind, leaning her head against his back, making it hard to concentrate on the matter at hand.

"Dinner will be a filet of beef with whisky butter, served with caramelized onions and roasted fingerling potatoes. As for dessert, I can whip us up an apple and pear crisp with toasted hazelnuts and dried cranberries, topped with a bit of vanilla ice cream."

"You spoil me, Angus." Her hands wandered, leaving him ready to chuck dinner and carry her off to bed.

"It's no more than ye deserve." He leaned over his shoulder and gave her a quick kiss, while basting the steak with butter. The tension he'd felt between them at the studio seemed a distant memory, making him a happy man.

"My mom would always take me apple picking in the fall. We'd bring home bags of apples and then spend the next week trying to find new ways of using them up. Crisp was always one of my favorites." She let out a long sigh. "Even though it was just the two of us, we did have each other and we made the best of it. I miss her, Angus. A lot."

"Och, love." The sadness and longing in her voice tore at his soul and heart. She had no family left, save for a father she didn't know—and who in all likelihood didn't know about her. He thought about how he was trying to hold her back, but the truth was that he was basing his fears on decades old speculations. "I can't imagine how hard this has been on ye."

She shrugged, as if trying to shake off her sadness. "It's fine."

Except that it wasn't. The need to ease her pain was overwhelming. He had to do right by her, but he was damned if he knew how.

Needing to comfort her and ease his guilt, he pulled her close, and with an arm around her waist, kissed her slow and sweet. Then doing his best to clear his mind, lest she pick up on his unease, he gave her one more kiss, and then turned back to his cooking. "If ye'd like to have a seat in the dining room, I'll get the soufflés."

Angus did his best to keep conversation light during dinner. He didn't want to think of her father or the threat. Didn't want her to think of how her mother was gone. He just wanted them to enjoy their time together. Yet, part way through dinner, she sat there not really looking at him, their conversion rather one-sided, and her appetite—despite the food being delicious, if he might say so himself—diminished.

"We could go sit by the fire if you're not hungry." He found himself now playing with his own food, his appetite ruined.

"I'm sorry, Angus. This is why I'm no good with relationships." She reached out and gave his hand a squeeze. "I'm afraid I've ruined your delicious dinner with my sour mood."

"Forget about dinner. It doesn't matter. Come." Angus took her hand and led her to the living room, settling her on the sofa while he got a fire going.

His mind raced over his options yet again while he sparked the kindling aflame and poked at it. It was becoming clear he wouldn't be able to keep things from her for much longer. He needed answers and information, but had nothing new to go on.

With the fire going, he sat by her side and pulled her close, wrapping his arm around her shoulder so she snuggled against his side. "Things *will* get better, love." He'd make damn sure of it.

"What if you're wrong? I'm no closer to finding my father, and you've seen how the people in town look at us. They're not happy with the company you're keeping, and things don't seem to be dying down."

"Listen, love. I don't give a rat's arse what people think." He reached over and took her hand, needing her to know she wasn't alone in this. He could easily see her packing her bags and heading back to the States—and she probably would have already if it weren't for finding her father. "I know this has been hard for ye, love, but ye can't let other's dictate yer life—nor can ye base yer happiness on another."

"I know that, Angus, but—"

"But nothing. Ye bought that gallery and came here to start a new life, so do that." Frustration and guilt had him dropping his head in his hands. Didn't she see that she belonged in Dunmuir, belonged with him? Why couldn't she just be happy? "Ye'll be fine with or without yer father. Do ye hear me? Ye can't let him be the be-all and end-all to yer happiness."

She shook her head and glared at him, hurt in her eyes. "How can you say that when you know what it's doing to me?"

"Live yer life, Rowan, and stop hitting the pause button." He'd have to tell her. Little by little these lies were killing what they had between them. "I just want to see ye happy."

"And finding my father will do that. Why does it feel like you don't want me to find him? I'm not imaging it, am I? You *had* been supportive, Angus. But lately? I don't get what's happened." She shook her head and looked away. "Is this some weird way of trying to push me away? Is it because I've all but moved in and now you're getting panicky? If you think this is all a mistake and would rather go back to just being friends, then just say so. It'd be a hell of a lot nicer than picking fights with me over my father."

Of course the poor girl was confused about what was happening between them, grasping at straws, because she only had a small portion of the facts. It only made sense that she'd think it had to do with their relationship.

"Och, love… it's not that. And I'm sorry, aye?" How the hell had he made such a mess of things? He tilted her chin up to make sure she could see that he meant the words he spoke. "Ye mean the world to me, love. More than anyone. Don't ye see that?"

"I do, but then… I don't know. Things have felt a bit… odd between us. Strained. You're all I have here, Angus, but I need you to be honest with me if this isn't what you want."

"Listen to me, love. Ye've made me happier than I've been in a very long time, and to be honest, I've ne'er felt more whole than when I'm with ye. But I need ye to trust me. I need ye to know that I only want what's best for ye." He reached out and took her hand, pulling her close, his head spinning and his gut in knots. "Rowan… I love ye. And I know ye're not there yet, but I need ye to know how I feel. I need ye not to doubt what's between us."

He knew better than to expect her to reciprocate his feelings, and that was fine—he could wait, even if it felt like his chest was being squeezed in a vice. As long as she knew how he felt and that no matter what he did, he had her best interest at heart.

"Then help me find my father. If you want what's best for me, help me." She cupped his cheek and kissed him, but he was drowning in guilt. "Promise me. I need to know I have your support when it comes it to finding him."

"Rowan…" He inwardly cursed, desperately wanting to lie to her and finding that he couldn't.

Her cheeks flushed red and her mouth fell open as her breath caught. "Am I missing something, Angus?"

"No." He groaned. "Maybe. Och, Rowan… I need ye to trust me, love."

She pulled away. "I do trust you—which is why this is catching me off guard. What do you mean by *maybe*?"

He reached out to take her hand, but she pulled away. It felt like he was on a cliff and the ground was crumbling under his feet. By the gods, he was losing her, and he knew the longer he took to answer her, the angrier she'd be. He just had to hold onto the reason he was doing this. "I want ye to stop looking for him."

Her hands clenched into tight fists, her jaw tight. "Just like that—because you said so? Or are you going to tell me why? And don't give me that whole *live your life* crap."

There was no avoiding it. He'd have to tell her.

Relief washed over him with his decision made. "Aye, love. I'll tell ye everything, but I need ye to know that I've only ever had yer best interest at heart."

"Just tell me what the hell is going on, Angus." She spoke through gritted teeth as her gaze bore a hole through him. He swore he'd never seen anyone look so angry.

"It's about yer mother. I don't have many details, which is why I didn't want to say anything, but I think something or someone had her frightened and it was the reason she left Scotland. Before going, she refused to tell my mother and Gordon Stuart—Conall's da—who yer father was, but they both said she was scared, and she made them promise to not go looking into the matter."

Her eyebrows perked, and he knew he was in trouble. "Wait. What do you mean *Conall's da*? Did you go and see him? Without me?"

"Aye, love." He was doomed. It felt like his heart was being wrenched from his chest. There was nothing for it, though. He'd have to come clean now that he'd started. "I needed to know if ye were putting yerself in harm's way by searching for yer father."

Her face was scarlet and her jaw was clenched so tight, he was surprised she managed to get the words out. "That was *not* your decision to make, Angus."

"Aye, ye're right. But it was the only way to keep ye safe. Ye'd go looking for him even if it put ye at risk. And though ye may be fine with putting yerself in harm's way, it's *not* fine with me."

"*Not. Your. Decision.*" With her hands clenched into tight fists, and the anger pouring off her in waves, he half expected her to hit him—repeatedly. And he'd deserve it.

"There's more." Dread had it so he could barely breathe. "When we went to visit Imogen, I had a feeling she wasn't being honest. Thinking she might have information on yer father, I paid her a visit."

She swayed. "What did you do, Angus?"

He squeezed his eyes shut for a long moment to center himself. "I asked her why she was lying to us. She still didn't say, but I now know without a doubt that I was right, and she knows more than what she's telling us."

She shook her head. "How could you, Angus? Not only did you do all this behind my back, but to not say anything?" Her eyes shimmered in the firelight as she blinked back tears. "What else have you been keeping from me? What else have you been lying about?"

He wanted to pull her in his arms, to comfort her, yet he couldn't when he was the source of her pain. "I asked Conall to look into Imogen and her background. Her family. She's hiding something. I just don't know what."

She blinked, and her tears spilled over. "I've got to go."

"Wait, love." He grabbed her hand before she had a chance to stand. "There's more."

"I can't. I can't take anymore and frankly, I don't care." She stood and he stood with her, but he didn't release her hand, even as she struggled to get free. "Let go of me, Angus."

He had to make her listen—and then maybe she wouldn't go. "It's yer father, love. I don't think he knew that yer mother was pregnant."

CHAPTER
Fifteen

ROWAN COULDN'T BREATHE. Her world was spinning out of control, spinning out from under her. She was furious with Angus, but the last words he'd spoken... She felt like the wind had been knocked out of her, leaving her numb and confused. He pulled her into his arms and sat them back onto the sofa—and she let him. Damn it.

"He doesn't know?" She was helpless to keep her tears from spilling over. Her entire life, she'd felt slighted and unworthy of her father's love and attention, as if she hadn't been good enough for him to bother with. No matter how hard she tried to stay positive, there was always a small part of her that felt incomplete and unwanted.

"I don't know if that's still the case, but my understanding is that yer mother never told him about ye, and she left soon after. He may still not know, love. But my concern is why yer ma never told ye his name and never told him about ye." Angus took her hands in his, his gaze kind yet intense. "She was frightened love—and if it's because someone didn't want yer father to know ye exist, then the threat might still be there."

Rowan's mind raced and her stomach churned as if she might be sick. It was all too much. She couldn't breathe. Couldn't think. "I need to go. I can't stay here."

When she stood, he stood with her. "Ye can't, love. It's not safe."

"Thank you for making yet *another* decision for me. Because I'm obviously not capable of a single thought without your help." Her entire body was shaking, too angry to even shed tears. She was ready to murder him. "How long have you known?"

He let out a ragged breath. "A few weeks—or more."

She shook her head and headed for the door, unable to even look at him, her stomach churning from the heartache.

"Rowan, please." He grabbed her arm, but she yanked it out of his grip and spun on him.

"*Don't*. Don't even speak to me, Angus." Her things, her bag. She didn't care. As long as she had keys, she could come for the rest later. She just needed to go. Needed fresh air. And needed to get away from him.

He stepped in her path, blocking her way. "Damn it, Rowan. Don't ye get that it could be dangerous? Yer mother didn't tell ye about yer father for a reason. Stop and think. Please, love. From what I've been told, yer father's a good man, but if he didn't know she was pregnant, then who had her so scared? What if they're the ones behind the threatening note?"

"You don't get it, do you? I'm not going to stop looking for him, Angus—especially if he doesn't know I exist. And I get that you're only trying to protect me, but you crossed the line when you started looking into this on your own and *didn't tell me*." She squeezed her eyes shut to keep the tears from falling. How did it all go so wrong—yet again? She felt hollow. As if her soul had been torn from her and she was nothing but an empty shell. "*I trusted you*, Angus. And you kept this from me—even though *you knew* how important it was to me."

"Och, love. I'm sorry. I only did what I thought was best."

"I know." She shook her head and looked away, her heart breaking. "But it's still over. I can't be with someone I can't trust. And I don't trust you, Angus. I don't know if I ever will."

When the incessant pounding on her cottage door refused to stop, Rowan dragged herself out of bed, her head spinning from lack of sleep and her eyes swollen from the tears she'd shed. If it was Angus, she'd murder him. Plain and simple.

"Lovely." She groaned and let Conall in. "It's a bit early for visiting, no?"

"Maybe if ye were still in Vermont, what with the time difference, but around here, lunch has come and gone, my dear." He wandered into her sitting room and took a seat.

"What are you doing here, Conall?" Couldn't he see that she didn't want company? She'd yet to sit, but when he motioned to the empty seat with a tilt of his head, she tossed herself in it.

"I'm here to take ye to my father. Angus called and said ye should speak to him." Conall tilted his head as he looked at her, his lips pursed. "Have to say, as smitten as Angus is with ye, I hadn't expected him to screw up this early on. The boy has a talent for that sort of thing."

She crossed her arms in front of her chest. "I'm not talking to you about my relationship. And what? You now do Angus's bidding. Can't say I expected *that* one."

Conall shrugged, not rising to her bait. "He promised to train that crazy mutt of mine in exchange. Now get showered and dressed. My father's waiting."

She took in a deep breath and let it out slowly while getting to her feet. "Are all Scottish men this bossy or is it something in the water of Dunmuir?"

Not waiting for a response, Rowan made her escape. She quickly showered and got dressed, taking the time to towel off her hair well before twisting it up and out of the way. Though she was still annoyed that Angus was interfering—obviously the man couldn't help himself—she was glad for the opportunity to speak to Conall's father. She didn't have many connections to her mother and her past, and now that things were over with Angus, she didn't know how any of the locals would feel about her.

Her heart ached to think of Angus, but along with the pain came her anger and hurt. Of all the people she thought she could trust... of all the people she didn't think would break her heart.

With her eyes burning, she took a deep breath and another, pushing her emotions back. She already looked a wreck with her eyes puffy and red, and didn't want to make matters worse by shedding fresh tears. With shaky hands, she swiped some gloss across her lips, took a moment more to settle herself, and then headed downstairs to where Conall was waiting.

"Ready. Are you driving or should I?" She tossed on her jacket to keep the chill at bay.

"I like my life, thank ye very much. Seeing as ye haven't been driving on our roads long and yer eyes are all but swollen shut from crying, I think it best if I drive."

She shook her head and ground her teeth. "You really know how to make a girl feel special."

"I do try." He pulled the door open with a smile. "After you."

It was a short drive down along the coast to a good-sized traditional cottage. Wrapped around the house were the bones of what would be a pretty garden come spring, the sea and sky acting as an ever-changing backdrop.

She stopped Conall with a hand on his arm. "Are you sure about this? I can't imagine your father wants to go digging up his past."

"I called first, and truth is, he'd like to see ye." Conall started to move towards the house, but Rowan stopped him again.

"Wait. Why did Angus want me to speak to him?" She didn't know what his motivations were anymore. Was he trying to prove something? Or was there more information he hadn't given her.

"How would I know? If ye want to know the inner workings of Angus Macleod, then ye'll have to ask him. Now are ye coming or not?" Behind his scruffy stubble, she could see his lips were pursed with impatience.

"It's a wonder you're still single when you ooze such charm."

Conall scoffed. "Aye—and that's the way I like it."

With a quick knock at the door, he didn't bother waiting, but rather let them in and led them to the sitting room. "Da. This is Rowan Campbell. My father, Gordon Stewart."

Gordon got to his feet and took her hand in his, his gold eyes intense as he held her gaze. "It's a pleasure to finally meet ye, lass. Please, have a seat."

Rowan pushed back her nerves and gave him a smile, noticing the similarities between the two men. "I can't thank you enough for seeing me."

She and Conall sat on the sofa across from his father, but she wasn't quite sure what to do with herself.

Gordon shook his head, his gaze returning to her time and again. "By the gods, ye look just like her."

She suddenly felt guilty, knowing her mother had hurt him. All she could do is hope that time had healed his wounds. "I'm sorry if this is awkward for you."

"Dinnae fash, lass. I'm glad ye came." There was such kindness in his eyes; it had her throat going tight. "How can I help ye?"

There was no point to delaying the matter, and at least now she felt more comfortable asking him. "It's my understanding Angus came to see you about my mother?"

"Aye, lass. He said ye were looking for yer father, and wondered if I might have information on him. Unfortunately, Iona didn't tell me much, given the circumstances." He shook his head, his lips pressed together.

"Angus wanted to know if she seemed scared, and I'll admit, Iona was certainly more frightened than I'd ever seen her."

Just like Angus had said. "I don't suppose she said why she was scared?"

"It had to be related to the pregnancy. Thinking back on it, I believe it had to do with his family. Whether or not that's who had her frightened or if it was the awkwardness of the situation, I couldn't say. But for her to not tell the lad she was pregnant... there'd have to be a damn good reason for it. She wasn't the flighty or frivolous sort, as I'm sure ye know, so she'd have thought the matter through."

So Angus had been right—not that it was any justification for what he'd done. But what happened to frighten her mother enough to leave the country without ever telling Rowan's father she was pregnant? She had to try and find him—now more than ever.

"I don't suppose you know any of her friends from college? We saw her roommate, Imogen, but she didn't have any information. Even a name would be helpful... anything at all." It was her last hope. She was running out of avenues for information.

"She was popular enough at university, even if Anne was still her closest friend. There was her roommate, as you said, though I'm not sure how close they were." He sat back with a sigh. "I hate to admit it, but it was hard to not get jealous when she was so far away and there were so many other lads constantly lingering. Not that I could blame them. She was a pretty thing, with a smile that set everyone at ease. And smart too."

He continued with a sigh that left Rowan's heart aching for the poor man. "I knew she wasn't truly in love with me, but I asked her to marry me anyway. I don't think she had it in her to turn me down since we'd been good friends and she loved me in her own way. It was before she'd left for university, and we were both so young."

Rowan could see it all unfolding, and heard the pain and longing that still lingered in Gordon's voice. "It didn't excuse what she did."

"No. It didn't. But I tried my best to understand." He shook his head with an exhale. "She loved him, ye know—yer father—and said he was a good man. Which is why I couldn't fathom her decision to keep the pregnancy a secret. I'm sure she had her reasons, but I couldn't tell ye what they were."

"And there's no one else who might know?" Her heart was aching, her hope dwindling.

"I wish I had answers for ye, lass. I truly do." Gordon picked up a shoebox that was sitting on the side table and handed it to her. "I found some photos from around that time. Thought ye might like them, though I doubt ye'll find any clues. Still, some of them are of her friends, though I wouldn't know their names. They were taken the few times I went to visit her in Edinburgh."

Knowing now that she might never find her father, a glimmer of hope and wishful thinking blossomed in her chest, as she reached over and touched Gordon's arm. "I don't suppose there's any chance you might be..."

He covered her hand with hers, his voice gentle and raw with emotion. "There's nothing I would like more, lass, but I'm afraid not."

Once at Conall's, Rowan sat on the sofa next to him and watched him type away on his laptop, his gaze locked on the screen. "What are you looking for?"

"Give me that picture—the one taken the day yer mother graduated from college." He took it from her and he looked at it again. "I'm thinking that anyone close to her might show up in this picture. There's her roommate and her family, by the looks of it. But there are also a few others here. If I can track down the list of those who graduated that day, I may be able to place names to the faces for ye."

Hope once again flooded her heart, even though she told herself it was a long shot. "Do you really think you can find out who they are?"

"Aye. Ye'd be surprised at the sorts of pictures people post of themselves online. Seems like everyone wants to reminisce about their past. When they were thin and young and had more hair. They all want to recall better times—not that they remember the reality of it."

She had to laugh. "You're awfully cynical for one so young, Conall."

He glared at her for a quick second before returning to his laptop. "Off with ye. Ye're distracting me, and I like to work alone. I'll stop by with any information I find."

It had been over a week since Rowan's argument with Angus, and one would think that with her gallery opening tomorrow, she'd have plenty to keep her busy. Yet somehow, despite her best efforts, Angus kept niggling his way back into her thoughts. Not that she'd seen hide nor hair of him. For someone so in love, he hadn't bothered to stop by or call to see how she was doing.

She knew from the start that it'd be a mistake to pursue anything serious with him, and yet he'd been impossible to resist. Even now, the mere thought of him had her heart beating a little faster, her stomach fluttering and her heart aching. Damn it.

Part of her tried to reason that he'd only been trying to protect her. Yet he'd been dishonest and kept things from her, manipulating things as she searched for her father. She couldn't trust him. If he'd given her the facts, they could have worked together to figure something out. Instead, he'd treated her like a child and made the decisions for her when they were hers to make.

Her eyes burned, but she took a deep breath and pushed her emotions to the side. No good would come of thinking about Angus—not when things were a mess between them. Instead, she got back to work putting the finishing touches on the gallery.

She wanted—needed—everything to be perfect for the opening tomorrow, and could only hope it would help the locals get used to her. Her recent split from Angus, especially after such a short time together, had the townsfolk giving her all sorts of looks, from smug to downright angry—and she could just imagine what they were saying.

But there was more weighing heavily on her mind—especially given her mother's past. She was late. Not by a whole lot, but it was enough to have her counting days and replaying the nights she'd spent in Angus's arms.

There was no way in hell she'd be going to the local pharmacy to pick up a pregnancy test. The rumors would whip through town like stink from a skunk. With luck, it was nothing more than the stress she'd been under. A few more days though, and she'd be trucking it to Glasgow and a pharmacy where no one knew her.

Doing her best to ignore the feeling of impending doom, she got back to hanging up the last of her photos and printed out the brochure she'd designed for the classes she'd be teaching. With how-to's on pottery to jewelry, she tried to market it as a fun alternative for a night out with a friend. She'd already set up a website, contacted the local papers, and with the weather warming, she hoped there'd be an increasing amount of tourists.

It was well past dinnertime, and her stomach rumbled in protest. She could go to the pub, but the thought of dealing with Lara or running into Angus had her quickly dismissing it as an option. Not that going home to cook or reheat leftovers seemed like an appetizing prospect. Angus had spoiled her with his gourmet cooking. Now, it didn't seem like a proper meal if something wasn't souffléd, flambéd, or bruléed. She grabbed her purse and flicked off the lights as she wandered towards the door.

Glass shattered in the darkness as pain rained over her, and she slumped to the ground.

CHAPTER
Sixteen

A NGUS PUSHED THROUGH the crowd, his heart pounding as panic consumed him. Lara hadn't said much over the phone—only that Rowan had walked into the bar covered in glass and dazed. Where the hell was she?

He spotted Walter Ramsey, the local constable. There. Behind him in one of the booths.

As if sensing him, Walter turned and immediately slowed his progress with a hand to his chest, holding onto him so he couldn't get by. "Easy there, Angus. She should be fine, though ye should still have a look at her. She doesn't want to bother with the long trip to the doctors or to emergency care. Cut and bump to the head, and a few superficial cuts to her face and hands from the glass. It was a rock through the window of her shop, and if I had to guess, it also hit her in the head. Given the age of the building, the glass hadn't been replaced with the tempered kind, so when it broke, it shattered into sharp pieces."

Processing the information, Angus nodded and shoved past him, his control tenuous. He saw the cuts, the blood, and it had his anger boiling over. He stepped to her side, though she didn't look at him.

He took a deep breath and tried to maintain some semblance of calm, not wanting to upset her further. "Rowan... I'll need to have a look, love." His voice sounded strained even to his own ears, his body so tense it was vibrating.

"They shouldn't have called you." Her gaze settled everywhere but on him, and it was like a knife to his heart. "I just want to go home."

He tried to keep his tone level, but it didn't help that he was talking through clenched teeth. "You can either let me look at yer wounds here, or I can take ye to my home and examine ye there. But ye're not staying in yer home alone when someone's just assaulted ye."

When she finally looked at him, his heart jerked to a stop as her eyes locked on his, shimmering ponds of green. "I'm fine."

"For fuck's sake, Rowan. Ye're bleeding and might have a concussion—and that is *not* fine." By the god's, the girl would drive him to drink. "If ye'd stop being so stubborn, ye'd take the threats seriously. This is the second one, and it's an obvious escalation from the first. So even if ye're not ready to acknowledge it, I'm not willing to risk yer safety."

"Well, it's not your choice, Angus." She got to her feet, but she was still unsteady. "I have to go board up the window and clean up."

Lara stepped to her side. "We'll manage it. Don't go worrying about that. Just get yerself home—and let the poor man take care of ye. We'll get to the bottom of this, aye? No one does this to one of our own." There were sounds of agreement from around the pub. "Now get out of my pub. Ye're getting glass everywhere and Angus is liable to punch something—or someone. Both of ye—get out."

Rowan nodded. "Thank you, Lara." She then settled her gaze on Angus, as if knowing she couldn't win this fight. "Could you please take me home?"

"Aye, love." He put a gentle arm around her back and took her hand to steady her, should she fall.

Not wanting to argue that his home would be safer, he took her to her home—not that she'd be staying there alone, if he had any say in the matter. "Which room has the best light? I need to make sure I get all the glass out."

"My studio." Her gaze still refused to fall on him any longer than necessary, and it all but killed him. "I need to get changed first… the glass."

"Aye, love. I'll wait here." He was desperate to hold her close and comfort her, but he'd gone and ruined that between them. It'd nearly killed him to give her some space after their argument, to not call her or swing by her house or the gallery. But now, after seeing how distant she was with him, he wondered if it'd been the right thing to do. Maybe if he'd stuck around, he could have smoothed things between them, made her see why he'd kept things from her.

When she returned, dressed in tights and a loose flannel shirt, they headed to the studio. She flicked on the lights, and he put his medical case down on the table, getting out his supplies and laying them out so he'd have easy access. "If ye could sit, that would help. I should be able to take care of most of yer injuries, but if it's anything serious, I'll have to take ye to the emergency in Glasgow."

She sat down like he asked. "I'm fine. Just a bump and a few cuts."

"Which likely have glass in them." He quickly examined her, relieved to find most of her injuries weren't terribly bad, and would heal within the week. The cuts to her face were few, but there were more on her hands. "The cut on your head isn't too deep and won't need stitches as long as ye're careful with it. Ye'll want to ice the bump though." He flashed a light in her eyes to make sure she wasn't concussed and then moved on to her cuts. "I'll numb them up a bit to keep it from hurting if I need to go digging around."

She nodded and he got to work, doing his best to ignore that it was Rowan he was working on—to ignore the anger that had his gut in knots and his shoulder tight. He often got called in to handle small injuries, since the closest physician was over an hour away, but this was different. This wasn't someone accidentally cutting themselves while chopping onions. This was an attack—on the woman he loved.

He finished up by covering the cuts with an antibiotic ointment and bandages. "Will ye come stay in my guest room or should I go get my things so I can stay here on the sofa?"

"Angus... I'm fine. You don't need to babysit me." She looked away with a ragged sigh. "I appreciate your help, but I think it's best if you go."

Her words stung and made his heart ache. "Do ye hate me that much? I don't get it, Rowan. I've only ever tried to do what's best."

When she looked at him, she was blinking back tears. "I know—but it doesn't matter. Nothing's changed—I'm still trying to find my father, and you still want me to stop looking—which means I can't do this. It was a mistake to get involved in the first place."

"Do ye really think that?" He refused to believe she truly felt that way. He brushed her cheek and tilted her chin up so she'd be forced to look at him. "I don't believe ye, love."

He leaned in and brushed her lips with his in a slow, sweet kiss, his heart pounding with hope when she didn't pull away. Instead, she clung to him, her forehead pressed against his—even if it was just for a moment.

"Why are you doing this to me, Angus?" She pulled away and got up to pace.

He stepped in her path and ran his hands down her arm. "It's the only thing I can think of to make ye see sense—to make ye see that I love ye."

"Just go, Angus. I'm begging you to just leave me be." Her tears rolled down her cheeks, as her eyes pleaded with him.

"Och, love… I'm begging ye to forgive me." He brushed her tears away, his hand still cupping her face as he fought through his own fears and desperation. "Let me help ye find yer father. Let me keep ye safe."

"How can I? You knew how important it was to be honest with me after my ex lied and cheated on me. And I trusted you, damn it. You said wouldn't hurt me—and that's exactly what you did." She pulled out of his arms and took a step away from him. "I get that you were trying to keep me safe, but you lied to me and worse—you tried to manipulate the circumstances so that I wouldn't go looking for my father, despite knowing how important it is that I find him."

He clenched his jaw to bite back his response and then took a deep breath to calm himself before speaking. "You were just attacked, love. Do you think I was still wrong to keep things from you?"

"Yes, I do. Because keeping things from me and keeping me safe are *not* the same thing, Angus. And if you don't see that, then there's no hope for us." She crossed her arms in front of her chest, disappointment in her eyes.

"I *do* get it, love. It's just the thought of something happening to ye is enough to keep me from thinking straight." He shook his head, worried she'd never forgive him. "I ne'er said I wasn't an eejit, love."

Unable to let her go, he found himself closing the distance between them. When she didn't move away, he wrapped an arm around her waist and pulled her close, nuzzling her.

"Tell me there's still hope, my love. I promise to ne'er keep anything from ye again." He had to make her see what she meant to him. "I love ye, Rowan Campbell. Don't be the one to break my heart, love, for I don't think I'll e'er recover."

She melted in his arms, as his lips found hers and he kissed her as if there would be no tomorrow. Although she eventually pulled away from him, there was a renewed hope in his heart.

"Will you help me find my father—in earnest?" There was no waver in her gaze, and he knew this was his one chance.

"Aye, love. I'll help ye any way I can." He reached out and took her hand, giving it a squeeze. "And I'll do all I can to keep ye safe."

She nodded, but slowly pulled her hand free. "You can stay if you want—on the couch. And just for tonight."

Even if it was a small step, it was a step in the right direction. "Aye, love. As ye wish."

True to her word, Lara had gotten the broken glass cleaned up and the hole boarded. "They may need to order in the glass, but with luck it won't take more than a day or two. I've got the dimensions and will let the window glazer know." Angus let the tape measure slip back into its casing and followed Rowan inside.

Things were still a little uneasy between them and seemed to have reverted back to the way things were before they'd started dating. Still, it was a good start and Angus hoped he'd be able to win her trust back before long. "Will ye still open for the day, love? Or will ye put it off until the glass has been replaced?"

She leaned against her desk, her arms crossed in front of her chest. "I don't know. I wanted everything to be perfect, and it just feels… off. It's not exactly the opening I'd envisioned for my gallery."

He saw the dozen roses, black as night, blooming in a vase by her laptop, and immediately recognized them as the kind her ex would always send. "From Stephen?"

"Yeah. He came across the gallery opening after I posted it online, hoping to drum up some business and get the word out. I guess he's still feeling guilty about being a cheating ass." She shrugged. "They were too pretty, and I didn't have the heart to throw out yet another bouquet."

His chest tightened at the thought of her ex trying to win her back. But it also made him wonder. "Rowan, would he be the sort to try scaring ye into moving back to the States?"

"No. I can't imagine he would." Her response was quick, but her furrowed brow told him she was still thinking about it. "It's likely one of the locals, even if most of them are probably feeling bad after last night's incident. None of them were too happy with me after you and I split up. And that's saying a lot, since they didn't like me when we were dating either."

Being reminded of their short-lived relationship hurt, but he could push through it now that she was speaking to him once again. That had been the longest week he could ever remember. "I could see someone writing the original note, but I can't imagine anyone in town being nasty enough to put a rock through yer window, especially with ye standing right there, knowing ye'd get hurt."

"Which leaves us with your suspicions about my mother being scared." She chewed on her bottom lip. "I've had Conall digging around. Do you think his search may have tipped someone off?"

"Anything's possible, love. Did he find anything?" It soon became clear that if Angus couldn't keep her from searching for her father, then the next safest thing would be to find out who he was—and with luck the threat would go away once her father was made known.

She reached past him, their bodies brushing, as she grabbed a folder stashed near her laptop. "Here's everything, including the latest stuff Conall unearthed."

With the file open on her desk, he flipped through the pages. "Do ye mind if I borrow this for a few hours? There's a lot here, and I need to check in on Astro. He's got his dog door, but he's not keen on being left alone for long and I've yet to go home."

"Actually, you can keep the file. Conall emailed me everything, so I can just print another copy of the photos and information. Maybe you'll notice something I missed." Her shoulders slumped and she let out a weary sigh.

"Don't lose hope, love." He brushed a stray curl from her face and tucked it behind her ear, resisting the urge to kiss her, even if every ounce of him was desperate to. "We'll find him. It's only a matter of time."

She nodded with a sigh. "I hope you're right."

Once Angus got home and gave Astro some much deserved attention, he spread out the information Conall had dug up. There was a lot, though most of it seemed to be centered around the day of Iona's graduation. A list of classmates was included, and luckily, the nursing program had been relatively small. There were a handful of men on the list, leaving him to wonder if one of them was Rowan's father. He scoured through the pictures next. There were several of Iona and her roommate, as well as photos with her other friends—even his mother.

Rowan really did look so much like her mother. The similarities were incredible, from the red hair and large almond shaped eyes, to the incredible cheekbones. Yet he could also see the differences—the things she got from her father. Her eyes were green instead of her mother's brown, she had a stronger jaw, fuller lips and her curls were looser and a more vibrant red.

Thoughts of his genetics class filtered through his brain, though it was hard to predict things like hair and eye color. The variations were just too many. Not even brown eyes on the father's side could be ruled out if there were recessive genes from both of the parents, though it would be less common.

It then occurred to him that Rowan had been looking at the photos to find friends of her mother's with the hopes they'd know who her father is. But maybe Rowan's father had shown up at the graduation and was right there in the pictures.

Angus flipped through the images looking for any resemblance between Rowan and the men in the photos. Sorting through the photos, he put them into piles. Some he thought he could safely dismiss, others weren't so easy.

His gaze was drawn to a photo of Iona with her father and Imogen with her family, taken at their college graduation. Conall had labeled everyone in this photo—from Imogen's father and mother, to her brother and sisters. Though Angus only knew Imogen and her brother as middle-aged adults, he could see the people he'd met in their younger selves.

He flipped through a few more photos, when something caught his attention. It was a photo of Iona arm and arm with a young handsome man with striking blue eyes and honey brown hair. Iona looked up at him with a sweet look, and Angus had to wonder. Only one problem—he didn't have a clue as to who the man was. His mother might know though. Just had to see a patient first.

CHAPTER Seventeen

I N DESPERATE NEED of caffeine, Rowan was ecstatic that she'd managed to acquire the espresso machine along with the gallery. The aroma of freshly ground coffee filled the air as she brewed a double shot of espresso and steamed some milk for a latte. Used to a steady dose of caffeine, she'd been going through withdrawal while trying to survive on the occasional cup, leaving her head in a fog.

With a mug of frothy heaven in hand, Rowan printed out new copies of the pictures Conall had sent her. There were new pictures she had yet to study, and with things better between her and Angus, she felt a renewed energy and hope. She could tackle looking for her father again—and she would find him.

Some of the photos were of her mother and Anne, others of her mom and Imogen, and then even more with people they'd yet to identify. She poured over the information, trying to match names with faces, but it was like walking through a blinding fog. She didn't know what the hell she was looking for.

Maybe if she cast a wide enough net, something would turn up. Finding the list of students her mother graduated with, Rowan started to make some calls. Some numbers were disconnected, but she also left several messages, including one for Imogen. Though Angus didn't think she was being completely honest with them, Rowan thought she was still their best bet. If anyone knew what her mother was up to while in college, it would be her roommate and friend.

She debated driving over to pay Imogen a visit, but after Angus accused her of lying to them, she doubted she'd be welcome—thank you very much, Angus. Yet... what if he was right? Why lie though? Maybe it was something that would put Rowan's mother in a bad light and she didn't want Rowan to find out. Or maybe the poor woman wasn't lying at all, but instead was simply a very private person and uncomfortable discussing her past.

Going through all the pictures, Rowan pulled the ones of Imogen and her family. Some were decades old, taken while she and her mother were at college, and others were more recent, clearly photos that Conall had found online, most of them related to business articles or the news.

Imogen had two sisters and one brother—the man who nearly plowed her over. There had also been a tragedy, taking their oldest brother away from them when he was only nineteen. A boating accident off the coast of France.

More recently, the father's health had deteriorated, his heart weak. With the company head in ill health, there were reports of turmoil within the firm. Rowan wondered if the argument they'd stumbled on between Imogen and her brother had to do with the future of the family business. What was his name? She found the page with the family information. There. Rory Murray.

She looked at the pictures again, easily finding Rory with his good looks and strawberry blonde hair. His hair had darkened towards more of a chestnut color as he'd gotten older and gone grey at the temples, though it only served to make him look more dignified. She went through the most recent pictures Conall sent over. There were several more of her mother with Imogen and her family, taken on graduation day. Imogen's father looked put out and annoyed for having to be there, despite it being his daughter's big day.

Again, her gaze traveled back to Rory. To her mother. In each picture, there was something… a certain tension. As if they were avoiding looking at each other, yet couldn't help but be drawn together.

She picked up the phone and dialed Imogen again. Once more, no one picked up and she was forced to leave a message. "Imogen… It's Rowan again. I'm sorry to keep bugging you but I have a question about my mother—and your brother. Please… call me as soon as you get this message."

She hung up and returned to the pictures, her fingers running over them—over Rory's face. Was she just seeing things out of desperation? Or was there really something between them? Rory… Rowan… even his name. They were both derived from the Gaelic for red. Was it her mother's way of linking her to her father in some small way? Or was she being delusional? Grasping at straws.

With her heart pounding and her gut in knots, she took a deep breath to try and calm her nerves. Her gaze strayed to Rory again and she was forced to blink back tears. Could it really be him? Was she looking at her dad?

She shook her head clear and got to her feet to pace, her thoughts refusing to slow. When that didn't help, she knew heading outdoors to take some pictures would help clear her mind and calm her thoughts. Double-checking her phone to make sure the battery was charged and the ringer was on, she grabbed her camera and wandered towards the seaport.

The fresh salt air filled her lungs, the scent of it pungent, as the air whipped around her, feeding her excitement. It made her feel alive, the energy of the sea palpable as the waves crashed on the rocks by the port.

She took frame after frame, knowing each one would give her more material for her gallery. Anything seemed possible now, and though she kept herself busy with work, a renewed hope bubbled in her chest, leaving her lightheaded. More than ever before, she felt as if knowing her father might finally become a reality.

Her phone rang and she quickly answered it, panicked they'd disconnect before she hit the right button. It was Imogen—she wanted to get together. To talk. She wasn't far from Dunmuir and would swing by the gallery within the hour.

This could be it. She might finally get the answers she was looking for—or she would once more be disappointed.

Pushing that thought away, she tried to stay positive and headed back to the gallery. Needing to tell someone, she immediately thought of Angus, but her call went through to his voicemail. She tried one more time, but still didn't have any luck getting through, so she left a quick message. He was probably knee deep in muck and wrestling a pig. The thought had a smile jumping to her lips—and left her wondering how he'd managed to finagle his way into her good graces in such short order.

The minutes trickled by as she waited for Imogen to arrive, leaving her nerves on edge. Trying to distract herself, she kept busy by sorting through the photos.

With the door to the gallery unlocked in anticipation, Imogen gave a quick knock and let herself in. Like before, her mother's roommate seemed very put together, her slacks perfectly pressed and not a hair out of place. And yet, there was a tension in her shoulders, and a tightness to her jaw, despite the smile perched on her lips. "I must admit, I was surprised to get your message."

"Thanks for coming by. Can I get you a cup of coffee?" Imogen politely declined, so Rowan got to the point. "As you know, I'm still looking for my father. A friend managed to find some pictures of my mother's graduation, and since you were in a lot of them, I was hoping you might be able to identify some of the people and shed some light on my mother's relationships with them." She picked up the file and handed it to her, hoping she'd help.

Imogen opened it and quickly paged through a handful of the pictures, before closing the file and holding it against her chest. "I'd love to help you with these. Perhaps we could do it over a late lunch? I got stuck in meetings most of the day, and I'm famished. There's a great little place just a few towns over."

Rowan supposed that someone as wealthy as Imogen probably didn't frequent the local watering hole for some pub grub. "That would be great."

Imogen looked around the gallery as Rowan grabbed her bag and jacket. "It's a lovely gallery. Pity about the glass. I see you cut yerself too. I hope it was nothing too serious."

"Just a few scratches. The locals don't take too kindly to strangers, I guess. Not that I'm going anywhere." Rowan felt her stubborn streak kick in, anger over the incident sparking deep in her chest. "I don't care much for bullies or being pushed around."

"No. I can't say I abide by them either. Still, one must do whatever it takes to keep themselves and their loved ones safe." Imogen wandered towards the door. Once Rowan had locked up the gallery, they headed out into the fresh air. "I think your mother knew that lesson well enough."

Rowan thought about what Angus had said—about her mother being scared. Thought of why her mother didn't tell her about her father. "I think so. She was a great mom, even if she did leave me with this mystery to solve."

"Well, I'm sure she had her reasons, my dear." Imogen led the way to where she'd parked. "I can drive since you're still new to the area."

Rowan paused, thinking of her mother who'd been scared enough to keep her father's identity from her. Surely she hadn't been scared of her roommate. Still… Rowan started to get a weird feeling. "Maybe the pub would be a better option? I have work I need to get to, and you said you were starving. The food really is quite good."

"On second thought, maybe you should drive." Hard silver caught the light as Imogen stepped to Rowan's side and grabbed her arm, discreetly sticking a gun in her side, sending Rowan's heart pounding. "I really don't want to hurt you, my dear, so please just get in the car. I'll give you the answers you're looking for and then we'll come to an agreement. Refuse to cooperate, and you and those you love will pay the consequences. There's too much at stake for you to ruin everything."

Rowan was taken aback by how cool and calm Imogen was, especially when her own heart felt like it was jumping out of her chest. She supposed that was the difference between holding the gun and being on the barrel end of it.

Her mind raced as she tried to figure out what to do, but Imogen had already shoved her in the car, and Rowan found herself pulling out into traffic, Imogen's gun pointed right at her. Rowan told herself not to panic. Doing her best to ignore her thready pulse and shallow breathing, she instead tried not to get herself killed via bullet or oncoming traffic. Maybe if she got Imogen talking, she'd have a better idea as to what was going on and how to get out of it.

"Are you going to tell me why you're doing this?" Rowan glanced at Imogen, her eyes immediately dropping to the gun before returning her attention to the road.

"You just had to keep snooping. If you'd left the matter alone, I wouldn't be forced to take such extreme measures." She shook her head.

"It's your brother, isn't it? Your brother, Rory, is my father." She hated that her voice cracked with emotion. "I'm right. Aren't I?"

Imogen refused to acknowledge Rowan's questions and all conversation between them ceased except for the directions Imogen occasionally doled out. Rowan had no clue as to where they were or where they were going, and though she had her phone, it was in her bag, which Imogen had grabbed and tossed into the back seat.

She tried again to get some answers. "Please. At least tell me why you're doing this. I know you don't want to hurt me. Please. Just let me go."

"You're right—I don't want to hurt you, but you cannot exist. If you'd just left things alone, you wouldn't be in this mess. But you just had to keep snooping around and looking into our affairs." She poked her with the gun. "Now keep quiet and drive, before I lose all patience, and you make me forget your mother was a friend."

"Or I make you forget that you're my aunt? Just say it. Tell me, damn it." Frustration threatened to choke her. She needed answers. If anything happened to her... she had to know who her father was. "I'm Rory's daughter—aren't I? He didn't know my mother was pregnant at the time. Did he ever find out? Does he know I exist?"

"Just keep driving, my dear. I'll tell you everything once we get there."

CHAPTER
Eighteen

"The analgesic will help him with the pain, but ye're to call me if it gets any worse or if he still feels uncomfortable." Angus handed Mrs. Tierney the bottle of medication and then gave the young terrier a good scratch, even as the pup tried to gnaw on his hand. "You. Stop chasing things ye shouldn't be chasing, and ye won't get kicked. Or mauled. Or whatever trouble it is ye're always managing to get into."

"He is a troublemaker, I'll give him that." The humor in her voice mingled with annoyance at yet another vet visit. "How's that lass of yer's doing. Heard she had problems with her shop. Pity that—and expensive too, I'll bet. I can't believe they put a rock through her window. In all my days, I've not seen anything of the sort. And to Iona's lass, no less. Poor girl. Don't know what the world's coming to."

"Well, hopefully that'll be the last of her troubles." Angus gave the old woman a bit of a smile, happy to hear that not everyone was unsympathetic. If anything, the incident seemed to have squashed some of the hostility. It was one thing for people to give Rowan looks and to gossip, but she'd been hurt in the process and it seemed to have knocked the sense back into their heads. These were good people—they'd just needed to be reminded of it.

It was one step in the right direction, yet on his way to see his parents, there was an undeniable knot in his gut that refused to slip free or be ignored. He knew his parents had likely heard the rumors—*all* of them. And since he'd avoided paying them a visit, he was sure he'd get an earful. Good thing he'd be able to keep them occupied by bombarding them with questions about the pictures.

Steeling himself for a lecture, he slipped in the front door, knowing his mother would likely be in the back of the house with a sharp tongue. He found his father sitting in his chair with a book in his lap. "Da."

His father shook his head, his lips pursed. "If ye were thinking that staying away would save yer arse, ye'd be mistaken. She's in the kitchen. And a good thing ye're too old for her to tan yer hide. Off with ye, laddie."

With his face already red, he left his father and wandered towards the kitchen. Best to cut her off before she had a chance to launch into a lecture.

"I need yer help, Ma." He went to her side where she was stirring something in a pot, and kissed her cheek. "I've got some pictures I need ye to look at."

She waved her spoon at him. "Angus Macleod. I thought I taught ye better than that. The things people have been saying. And don't go trying to tell me they're untrue. I know what ye're like when ye get yerself all riled up. I can't believe ye hauled the poor girl onto yer shoulder. Ye best show some respect, or I'll be forced to remind ye of yer manners."

"Aye, Ma." He tried to hide his grin, but couldn't help himself, and was forced to jump back as his mother took a swipe at him with the wooden spoon.

"Quit being cheeky." But already he had her smiling. "Now, what is it ye need help with? And what is this about Rowan being hurt by broken glass?"

"She's all right, Ma. The cuts weren't too deep. As for yer help… it's about these pictures. I tried to keep Rowan from looking for her father, but I can no longer do it. It's put a wedge between us, and truth is, I think she has a right to know." He gave her the file. "Any help would be appreciated."

"I'm sorry if I caused problems between ye. It was ne'er my intention." She touched his arm, and then sat down at the table, managing a tentative smile. "Let's see what we have then."

Opening the file, she flipped through the pictures, her brows pulled close as she closely looked at the photos. "Where on earth did ye get these?"

"Conall worked his magic. Managed to find some of the photos online, and then his father dug a few more of them out of the attic."

"Conall, aye?" She looked up from the photos, an eyebrow perked and humor sparking in her eyes.

"Aye. He's agreed to help Rowan, so I can't fault him." He reached over and pushed aside some of the pictures to find the one he wanted. "Do ye know this man here?"

"Och, aye. That's one of Iona's cousins. Grew up in Manchester, but would come to visit during the summer."

Disappointment left his heart heavy. He was hoping to have some new leads, if not answers for Rowan.

Anne picked up one of the graduation photos. "Now this one here… that was her roommate, wasn't it?"

"Aye. Imogen Murray. We went to speak to her, but I swear, Ma, she was lying to us about something. Just wish I knew what she was keeping from us. Conall mentioned they're a private family, but I think it was more than that." He looked at the photo again.

Maybe it was the awkward angle he was viewing it at, but something seemed to fall into place. "Ma… what do ye know about this fella here? His name is Rory Murray."

The color drained from her face. "Did ye say his name was Rory?"

"Aye, Ma. What is it? Is that him?" Angus's heart pounded against his ribs, his pulse echoing in his head.

She picked up the photo and looked up at Angus, her face blank with shock. "Early on, when Iona first went away to university, she'd mentioned meeting her roommate's brother. It had escaped my memory, but I remember thinking that she seemed quite taken by him, even though she'd only met him the handful of times he'd gone there to see Imogen. And then, it seemed like she stopped talking about him altogether. I know it's not much, which is why I hadn't thought of him, but looking back on it… I don't know. There was something in the way she spoke of him when they first met. I could be mistaken, but… it could be him, Angus."

"And if he's the one we're looking for, then we know why Imogen was lying to us."

"As powerful and wealthy as that family is… I can see why Iona was worried. People with an abundance of money and power tend to get protective of it. They may see Rowan as a threat—and if they're the type to keep to themselves, they'll not want an outsider coming in and demanding a piece of the pie."

Angus got a sinking feeling in his gut. "But Rory didn't know of Rowan, according to Conall's father."

She tapped the photo on the table, distracted. "Maybe not. But just because Rory wasn't told of the pregnancy, doesn't mean Iona didn't tell her roommate."

"If Imogen is still trying to keep it from her brother, then it would be a reason to lie to us." The pieces were slowly falling into place, and it left him fighting to slow his pulse as the feeling of dread overwhelmed him. "Bloody hell. The threats… I don't think they were from the locals."

Angus cursed when he finally made it into an area with reception and realized that Rowan had called. He retrieved the voicemail while cursing. *"Call me. I think I know who my dad is, Angus. I think it's Rory Murray— Imogen's brother. I've called her, but haven't heard back. Give me a ring, okay?"*

Damn it. Angus tried to call Rowan, worry filling him when he couldn't get through to her. With luck, she'd still be at the gallery, but not being able to get a hold of her had every muscle in his body locked up and his head spinning. He tried the store, tried her cell, tried her home, and turned up empty.

He found the yellow Mini, but there was no sign of her at the gallery. He tried her phone yet again, in case it was nothing more than spotty service. He left her a message, telling her to call as soon as she was able. Thinking she might be in the pub, he had no better luck there, but left a message with Lara. Where the hell had she gone, if her car was still in town? He tried the shops, but she was nowhere to be found. Desperate, he headed to her house. Still not there, panic consumed him.

Conall. Maybe he'd picked her up and they'd swung by his place. He pulled down the drive and pounded on the door until Conall pulled it open, fire in his eyes. "Is Rowan here?"

"Bloody hell, Angus. No. She's not here." Conall wrestled with the pup who was frantically trying to escape into the open air just beyond the threshold.

"I think she's in trouble. She figured out that her father's probably Rory Murray, but I haven't been able to track her down or get in touch with her." Angus ran a rough hand down his face, the words pouring out in his panic. "The Mini's still in town, but she's not there, and I'm worried she's gotten herself into trouble. Can ye help me find her?"

Conall stepped to the side, letting him in. "I bloody well hope so."

Angus told him all he knew and suspected, trying to keep his voice calm and failing miserably. "I don't know if I'm being paranoid, but given all we know, I can't rule out that something's happened."

"She's got a smartphone, aye? Give me her number." Conall jotted it down and started tapping away on his laptop. "Mind ye, if she's not in trouble, and I've just hacked into her accounts, I'll be blaming you for all of this."

"Just find her and I'll deal with her wrath when the time comes." By the gods, he didn't know what he'd do if anything happened to her. "Hurry. Please."

Each moment felt like a lifetime. Finally, Conall tapped at the screen. "The last signal was picked up south of here, not far from Glasgow."

"Imogen... she's just south of Glasgow. But Rowan can't be on her way to see her without a vehicle." Did Imogen come up to visit her? Or did she contact Rory directly? But would she go there on her own? None of it made sense. He got to his feet and grabbed his keys. "Can ye keep tracking her? And keep calling her too—I don't know that I'll have coverage until I get to the city."

"Aye. Keep me updated, and I'll do the same."

Angus got to Imogen's home in record time, only to find no one there. He pounded the door with his fist, taking one deep breath after another, as he fought to keep his head clear, fought to keep from thinking the worse.

He called Conall and was told Rowan's signal had vanished and Conall had been unable to contact her. At a loss of what to do next or where she might be if Imogen had her, he got desperate. "Do ye have Rory Murray's address and phone number?"

Jotting down the information, he got back on the road. At least Rory's address wasn't far from Imogen's, and Angus found himself pulling down the drive of a large home within the half hour. He pounded on the door, trying to push back his panic and still wondering all along if Rowan was sitting someplace safe, having a cup of coffee, while he raised hell to save her.

Rory answered the door, biting back his response and annoyance at the commotion when he saw Angus, recognition filtering over his features. "Ye were at Imogen's, were ye not?"

"Aye. Is Rowan here?" He tried to look past the man's shoulder, but couldn't see anything?"

Rory's brow furrowed in confusion. "The lass ye were with? No... I'm sorry, I don't understand what this is about, though I'll admit, the lass seemed terribly familiar." He stepped to the side to let Angus through. "Come in."

Angus followed Rory into the living room and took a seat, but was unsure if he was doing the right thing. Rowan should be the one to tell her father of her existence—if he was even right about that piece of the puzzle.

"I think Rowan's with yer sister. But that's just the start of it..." Angus took a deep breath, to steady himself. "Do ye know Iona Campbell?"

The color drained for Rory's face. "By the gods... I thought I was losing my mind. She's Iona's lass then?"

"Aye, she is. But there's more... I think ye're her father."

CHAPTER Nineteen

ROWAN WALKED INTO the seaside cottage, her heart racing in panic when she saw it was no longer just her and Imogen. There were two men, twice her size and looking like they'd do whatever was being asked if the price was right.

"I don't want to hurt you, my dear, but I have my priorities—and that's my family and the continued success of our company." With the men armed, Imogen was able to tuck away her pretty little gun. "Please sit. I want to come to an arrangement that will work for both of us."

Rowan spotted a phone on the wall, but knew she wouldn't be let anywhere near it. Her own cellphone had been tossed out the window after one too many calls annoyed Imogen. No doubt it was Angus trying to track her down. With luck he was now searching for her, though how he'd find her here of all places, she hadn't a clue. She'd tried to keep an eye on the street signs and landmarks, though she thought it unlikely that she'd get the opportunity to call for help.

With few options available, she turned her attention to Imogen. "If it's your money you're worried about, rest assured that I want no part of it. I've only ever wanted the chance to know my father. I don't care about the money or the business. That's not why I'm here."

Imogen pursed her lips, her legs crossed and her gaze hard. "That may well be the case, but that's not my concern. Your father—and yes, dear, he is indeed your father—needs to run the family business. My father worked too hard to build it up, and it would kill him to see Rory walk away and let it all fall apart."

"I don't see what that has to do with me. I won't interfere if that's what you're worried about." None of it made sense, and it had Rowan questioning just how sane Imogen was. It was bad enough to be kidnapped at gunpoint, but at this point, none of it even made sense.

"You see, the only thing keeping Rory at the helm is obligation and guilt. My father's health has deteriorated enough that he can no longer run things. If he finds out that our father sent Iona away, he'll turn his back on us. It would kill my father and ruin us. As good as Rory's been at dealing with the business, he never wanted it." She scoffed and shook her head. "As if he'd be able to pursue his art without our father's support. And it's not like your mother would have wanted him then anyway."

Anger flared in her gut. "If my mother loved him, then the money wouldn't make a bit of difference. She never married. Never even dated. So don't go telling me about my mother when you clearly didn't know her."

Imogen leaned forward, venom in her eyes. "If she loved him, then she would have stayed rather than take the money. Who do you think put food on your table and clothes on your back?"

"My mother worked her ass off, thank you very much. As for why she left—you tell me. Given that I'm being held at gunpoint, I can't imagine you and your father didn't issue your own threats. Did he threaten to disown his son if she told him?" Rowan saw the recognition in Imogen's eyes. "So he did. Maybe it was my mother who loved him enough to not ruin him. But there'd likely be more, right? Did your father threaten to harm my mom? Her family? Her friends?" It was a stab in the dark, but again she saw the acknowledgement in Imogen's eyes.

"And I'll make you a similar offer. Leave Scotland and never contact my brother. I'll make sure the deposits into your bank account will continue, and you and your friends will continue to live happy and healthy lives. Contact my brother, and you'll all suffer for it." She smoothed her dress pants. "Like I said, I don't want to have to hurt you, but I will if you push me."

"So… I agree, and what? You just let me walk out of here?" Doubtful. She had to find a way out of this mess—and if she was indeed pregnant, then it wasn't just her life on the line.

"If you agree, I'll have you escorted out of the country. My yacht is just off the coast here. You'll be taken away from here, and will eventually be allowed to make your way back to the States." Imogen sat there, her back straight, her hands linked in her lap, as if they were discussing the upcoming spring fashions over a cup of tea and cakes.

It was absurd. The whole thing was crazy. But she thought of Angus, and had no doubt Imogen was capable of sending some thug to his doorstep. "Just so I have this right… this is all so your brother will continue to run the business."

"And to keep my father from harm. His heart couldn't take the shock or strain of your appearance and the effect it would have. Rory never wanted to run the business, and that would have been fine, since it was our older brother, Niall, who was supposed to follow in my father's footsteps. But when Niall died, it fell to Rory, even if he was too selfish to want the responsibility."

Rowan remembered reading about the boating accident, and could see how it all played out. Rory would end up with the business falling on his shoulders as the next in line, whether he wanted it or not.

Imogen continued, as if lost in a past that had consumed her. "My father married Rory off to a competitor's daughter to seal a much needed deal, making it even more difficult for him to walk away, since he'd disappoint not only his father and family, but his wife and in-laws. You see, my father has always been good at getting what he wants, and though I have no head for business, we do share that particular talent." She let out a sigh, looking bored even in the absurdity of the situation. "I need a decision. Now. Because I'm growing impatient, my dear, and it would be far easier to just shoot ye and let ye disappear into the sea."

Stubbornness left her wanting to challenge Imogen—to tell her she was insane. The whole situation was just absurd. "I need some time to think about this."

Imogen scoffed. "What is there to think about, my dear? You can either live and those around you will remain safe, or I can shoot you. Perhaps it was a mistake to give you a choice. Gentlemen. If you'd be so kind."

CHAPTER
Twenty

A NGUS FOUND RORY's stash of whisky and poured him a glass while the poor man sat there on the sofa, not moving, his jaw slack and his face pale. No doubt it was a shock to find out you'd fathered a child close to thirty years earlier, never suspecting the truth.

"I always wondered why she left so abruptly." Rory took the glass Angus offered him, and mumbled his thanks before taking a long sip. "But why... Iona never said anything."

"I've been told by more than one person who knew her well, that she was frightened. I'd assume that had something to do with it." Angus ran his hands down his thighs in an attempt to uncurl his fists. "She never told anyone yer name—not even Rowan. And I'm sorry to say, Iona passed about a year ago."

"I can't tell ye how it pains me to hear it." Rory's shimmering eyes settled on the amber liquid in his glass. "And Rowan... she came looking for me?"

"Aye. She's spent the last six weeks trying to figure out yer identity. It's why we were at Imogen's that day—and it's why I think she's now in danger." Angus sat forward, trying not to shake the man into action. "Yer sister—would she have a reason for wanting to keep Rowan from ye?"

Rory nodded, finally looking up into Angus's eyes, a fire and intelligence there fueled by anger. "Aye, she would. I've been threatening to step down from running our company. If I found out that my father and sister somehow coerced Iona to leave—pregnant with my child—and then kept Rowan a secret from me, it'd be the last straw."

That gave Imogen motivation. "Would Imogen harm Rowan to keep ye from finding out?"

The poor man looked as if he'd been struck. "By the gods, I'd hope not, but the way she's been acting as of late, I wouldn't put it past her. We need to find them. Now."

Panic now threatened to consume Angus, but he had to push through it. Had to keep his head clear so he could think. "Give me yer sister's cell number. I've got a friend who might be able to track its location. If Imogen has Rowan..."

"Aye. Imogen's not been thinking straight. Even contacted lawyers to try and keep me in my current position." He went to his desk and jotted something down. "Here's her number. Call yer friend and see what he can do. I'll make a few calls of my own to see what I can find out."

Angus relayed the information to Conall, who said he'd call as soon as he managed to track Imogen's phone. Time seemed to be running slower than honey in the winter, and it felt like they were getting nowhere fast. If anything happened to her... he didn't know how he'd manage.

Rory hung up the phone. "She took the family yacht from where we keep it moored. I don't know where she's taken it or if Rowan's with her, but taking the yacht isn't something she'd normally do."

Angus answered his ringing cell within a second of the call coming through. Conall had come through for him. He jotted down the information as Conall relayed it. "Thank ye. Call me if they move from that location. Aye. We're on our way. I'll let ye know."

While Angus hung up with Conall, Rory looked at the address. "I know this place—we used to summer there when we were quite young. It was my mother's family cottage, though we've not been there in decades. It's about forty minutes from here. Should we call the police?"

"Depends. How do ye think yer sister will react to the police surprising her?" The last thing he needed was Imogen panicking.

"Aye, ye're right. We'll call once we're there. That'll give us enough time to try and get the situation under control, but will give us the backup we'll need if things don't go to plan. I'll make a few more calls to see if I can get more help." Rory already had his cell out as he followed Angus out the door.

Angus insisted on driving, not wanting to risk Rory being a slow driver. And though they were making good time, it still wasn't fast enough as far as Angus was concerned. He didn't dare think of what trouble Rowan might be in, knowing his mind would think the worse. He needed to stay positive. Needed to know he'd find her unharmed.

"What if ye call Imogen and tell her ye know of Rowan?" It was the only thing Angus could think of to try and get Rowan back safe.

Rory shook his head. "Aye, ye'd think it the logical conclusion, but at this point, I'd worry she might hurt the lass out of spite."

Angus didn't quite understand. "For what?"

"My eldest brother was groomed to take over for my father when he retired, but he died before he ever got the chance. Busy studying art, I had no desire to do it, even though I was good at it. Imogene on other hand had all the desire in the world, but her strengths lay elsewhere. She's only ever wanted to please my father and get his attention, but instead, my father insisted I run the company. It's made her bitter, aye?"

"And by the sounds of it, just a bit insane. I swear, if she hurts Rowan…"
He pounded the steering wheel, unable to bear the thought. By the gods,
he loved her. From that first email. That first kiss. There could be no other.

"We'll get to her, lad. And she has to be all right. I can't have anything
happen to her when she's only just come into my life. All those years
between us lost…" Rory looked down and shook his head, his shoulders
slumped. "I should have been there for her—and for Iona. I would have
given it all up for her, but she broke things off between us and left without
a word. Now I know why."

"Well, if I have any say in the matter, ye'll have plenty of time to make
it up to Rowan. We can't be far, aye?" They were near the coast, the salt
air filling his lungs. It should calm him, yet instead he found himself
fearing the dangers of the sea. Even a conditioned swimmer would have
a hard time keeping their head above water around here—if they didn't
freeze to death. And Imogen had taken the family yacht.

"Nearly there. I'm calling the police. They should get here shortly."
Rory gave the police their details and pointed Angus down a different
road. "That's the cottage in the distance."

"There's more than one car there—do ye recognize them?" Either
Imogen had back up or there were others involved.

"Just Imogen's vehicle. I don't know the other." They pulled up to the
cottage and got out, but before Angus could go charging in after Rowan,
Rory put a hand on his arm and held him back. "Let me go in first and
do the talking. I might be able to get her to see reason, aye?"

"Aye. But I'm telling ye now—Rowan's my priority. I'll do whatever
it takes to get her out of there safely."

Chapter Twenty-One

"Let go of me." Rowan tried to pull her arm free of the goon's grip, but
his fingers dug in, bruising the flesh as panic rose up in her chest. Unable
to think past the pounding of her heart, she brought her knee up to his
groin, her hit fueled by adrenaline. As he doubled over with a groan, she

brought her foot down on his instep. It was enough to loosen his grip. She got free, but the other guy grabbed her by the waist and lifted her off her feet as she screamed and lashed out at him.

"Stop it now or I'll shoot. Do you hear me?" Imogen held her gun in a shaky hand, her eyes narrowed and the tendons in her neck standing out.

As crazed as Imogen looked, Rowan slowed her struggles. The man put her down on her feet, and then transferred his grip to her arm to keep her from escaping. He gave her a hard shake, and Rowan took her chance, worried she wouldn't get another. As he shook her, she lashed out a flaying fist in Imogen's direction.

The gun went off and chaos erupted around them. The guy holding her ducked and let go. Rowan lunged at Imogen, tackling her to the ground when the door burst open.

Angus—and her father.

Seeing them distracted her enough to make a mistake. Another shot went off as Imogen struggled to get free, this time finding a mark.

Rory jerked backwards, his shoulder and chest erupting in red as he dropped to his knees. Rowan screamed and tried to make her way to him as Angus dove for the gun, beating one of the other men to it. Angus spun and pointed it at the guy, slowing him in his tracks as Angus got to his feet, a wary eye on the scene.

"The three of ye, to yer feet and yer hands where I can see them. And if ye think I don't know how to use a gun, ye're mistaken." Angus didn't take his eyes off them. The two men did as he asked, but Imogen was wailing and inching towards her brother, hesitating while Angus had a gun pointed at her. "Help's on the way, Rowan. Just apply pressure to the wound."

"I'm trying." Rowan's shaking hands were covered in blood as she leaned forward, using her weight to help stem the flow. He couldn't die. Couldn't. Not when he'd been taken from her all these years. Not when she'd just found him.

Rory reached up and brushed her cheek, his touch weak. "Dinnae cry, my darling lass."

She tried to shake the tears free, not even aware they'd fallen until he mentioned it. All that time lost, time she should have spent with him—and for what? The greed of people. So a father could force his son into the family business. So a sister could manipulate a situation.

When the sirens could be heard approaching, her tears turned to ones of relief. "Help's here. Just hold on."

"Forgive me, my dear. I wish I could have been there for ye." With his words spoken on a ragged breath, his eyelids fluttered shut.

Rowan took comfort in Angus's embrace, his strong arms holding her to him as they continued to wait, her father taken into surgery hours ago. She didn't know how she'd ever thank Angus for all that he'd done. The police had taken Imogen and the men she'd hired into custody. Worried as Imogen had been about her brother, she'd made a full confession to the police. Not that Rowan was ready to forgive her for nearly killing Rory and kidnapping her at gunpoint. Somehow, it wasn't exactly the family reunion she'd been hoping for.

And speaking of family—the police said they'd contact Rory's family, though he was divorced from him wife, and neither of his two sons lived in Scotland. Two brothers. She actually had family once again.

But how would they feel about her when she was the reason their father was fighting for his life? And what if they thought she was only after the family fortune and business? Would they think she was only there for her share of the money? Would they even accept her—or would they question the authenticity of her claim? With her worries pushing her towards desperation, she held onto Angus, and tried her best to keep her thoughts at bay.

It was another hour before the surgeon approached. Rowan sat up out of Angus's arms, her back stiff and her muscles wound tighter than rigging on a full sail. "He's out of surgery, and we were able to repair the damage, but he's lost a lot of blood. We're keeping him comfortable. Still, it'll be a while before he wakes, so I suggest going home and getting some rest. We'll call if there's any change."

She waited until the surgeon left before turning to Angus, knowing he'd want to take her home. Looking up into his blue eyes, she reached out and took his hand, the feel of it strong, capable. "I don't want to go."

"Och, love, ye need to get some rest. Ye've had a long day, and it won't do ye any good to wait here when there's no chance of him waking. We can stay in a hotel close by, and come back at the crack of dawn. Ye've likely not even eaten since this morning." He tucked a red curl behind her ear. "Let me take care of ye for a bit, and I promise to have ye back here first thing."

"What if he wakes and no one's here?" She closed her eyes to keep her emotions from overwhelming her. "I can't bear to lose him, Angus."

"Aye, love. I know. But ye'll want to be in good form when he awakes, and that won't happen if ye're neglecting yerself. With the medications they've given him, he won't awake tonight." His hand wandered to her cheek, his touch lingering as his gaze flicked to her lips.

She could see he wanted to kiss her, and more than ever, he meant the world to her, yet her life was still in an upheaval and he deserved better. He could have also been injured, and for something he'd tried to warn her about, no less. She just had far too much uncertainty in her life—and wondering if she was pregnant certainly wasn't helping matters.

As if he might read her thoughts, she looked away and took a step back. She couldn't imagine what he'd think if he found out she might be pregnant. Maybe she could get away for a few minutes and pick up a test. She was finally far enough away from Dunmuir to not be recognized. And if she got some answers, then maybe she'd feel a bit more settled. After all, she'd finally found her father.

"I guess you're right. And if we stay local, we can get back here early enough." She managed a smile, hoping to set him at ease, and then, unable to resist him when he was so near and needing to feel the solid comfort of him, she slipped her arms around his waist. "Thank you."

"Anything for you, love." He kissed the top of her head. "I don't know what I'd have done if I lost ye."

"I'm just sorry you've had to deal with so many of my messes. And *you*... you could have been killed today, and it would have been my fault." The thought of it had her gut in knots, her chest tight and tears stinging her eyes. "You'd be smart to get as far away from me as possible."

"Now, how could I possibly do that, love, when ye're my very heart?" He tipped her chin up towards him. "Look at me, love. None of this is yer fault—ye weren't the one with the gun, and ye weren't the one who put us in danger. That was Imogen. Do ye hear me?"

"I know." And she did—yet she still felt responsible. Still felt guilty.

"Do ye really?" He ran a hand down her arm and linked his fingers with hers, a sigh escaping his lips. "Let's get ye out of here. Maybe once ye get some rest ye'll see the reality of the matter."

Angus found them a hotel nestled in the outskirts of Glasgow. Thoughts of their room accommodations left her debating what she should do about him, but Angus didn't give her an option, and instead booked them two separate rooms next to each other. She was at once both relieved and disappointed.

"Are ye coming, love?" Angus looked at her, worry creasing his brow.

"Sorry. Just a bit distracted." She let him steer her towards their rooms, while she tried to decipher her feelings for him.

Truth was, if she stuck around—if she gave in to the feelings she had for him, she knew she'd be a goner. She'd fall heart and soul, head over heels with every fiber of her being in love with him. And that scared her. She'd been burned before, and she knew that if she let herself fall in love with Angus, she'd fall far harder than she had for any other man. That left her wanting to put on her racing shoes and find the nearest exist, her wounds from Stephen still too fresh to want to acquire new ones.

Yet the thought of being left alone with nothing but her thoughts had her tightening her grip on him as he saw her into her room. "Angus, I don't want to be alone."

"I can stay if ye'd like." He sat down on the bed. "Come, love, and rest yer head."

And so she did, curled up against his side, his strong arms holding her close until exhaustion swept her away into a mercifully dreamless sleep.

Come morning, her body felt like it'd been twisted like a pretzel and run over by a truck. She was hoping a good night's sleep would have settled her worries about Angus, but with uncertainty about her father's health looming, it only made her question things further.

Not having thought to bring a change of clothes to a kidnapping, she did her best to freshen up and then got ready to head to the hospital. "Are you ready to go?"

He pursed his lips as those knowing eyes of his took her in. "Aye, love. I'm ready, but ye have me worrying about ye. It's not just yer father is it?"

She wanted to groan. And curse. "Isn't that enough? I mean, what more do I need?"

"Is that really all there is, then?" His eyes narrowed as if scrutinizing every detail of her. "Because ye have a tendency to roll yer eyes for just a flicker of a moment when ye're trying to avoid discussing something."

"That's not true." The man was infuriating. "There's nothing bothering me other than my father being on death's door before I ever get the chance to know him."

"Och, lass, I get that ye're worried about yer da, but the eye roll ye just did again tells me there's more bothering ye." He took her hand and slowly pulled her to him, and though she resisted, it was only for a moment. "Tell me what else is on yer mind, love. Ye can trust me—despite all my screw-ups."

And then before she had a chance to think, before she found the strength and courage to deny him, she spoke the words she'd been keeping to herself. "I think I'm pregnant."

Angus swept her off her feet and twirled her around as he let out a whoop of joy—which only made her feel guilty that she couldn't be as enthusiastic about the whole thing. He finally set her down, and when he looked at her, his smile faded, his brows drawn.

"Och, love. Dinnae fash yerself. A bairn could be a good thing." He brushed her cheek, his touch gentle.

She let out a weary sigh and fought to keep the frustration from her voice, but failed miserably. "Yeah, it could be a good thing—when my entire life isn't in an upheaval. When I'm in a relationship—or married. Not when I'm single, in the middle of opening a new gallery, and just survived a kidnapping. So don't tell me not to worry—or fash myself. Because I'm *fashed* up to my eyeballs, Angus. And I can't do this. It was a mistake to think I could settle down and a have a normal life."

"Rowan, I get that this isn't ideal—and ye may not even be pregnant—but ye can't go panicking. Ye've ne'er been so close to getting what ye want, yet ye're getting ready to run again—just like ye always have." He looked away with a shake of his head. But when he looked back, it was with an intensity that stole her breath away. "Don't ye see... ye can be happy, love. Even if it's not with me—though I sure as hell hope it is—ye can't keep running if ye want to find happiness. Ye've got to take the bad with the good and stand yer ground—fight for yer happiness. It's the only way, love."

"Didn't I warn you? I'm no good at this, Angus." How many relationships had she ruined? He meant too much, and she couldn't bear to have the same thing happen between them. She started to turn away but he grabbed her hand, her emotions overwhelming her. "I just can't think of this right now. I need to get to the hospital."

"Very well. Let's get ye to yer father, though we're not through discussing this, love." He slipped an arm around her waist and pulled her close, her curves pressed against his solid form, his lips too close, his gaze intense. He had her head spinning as her breath hitched—and he looked ready to devour her. Brushing the hair from her face with his free hand, his touch lingered, and then he kissed her once, twice, and then again in a thorough exploration, until she clung to him, her hands fisting his shirt.

When he pulled away, they were both breathless. "I'm not going to let ye run, love. I'll be here by yer side as a friend or lover, and I'll always have yer back, no matter what problems arise. But we'll deal with them. Ye don't get to take the easy way out. Ye don't get to run."

He was right. Damn it. She couldn't let history keep repeating itself, nor could she let her past and her insecurities keep getting in her way. She took a deep breath and gathered whatever courage she could muster. He deserved better—and so did she. She deserved to be happy. And it was a start.

She steeled herself and got ready to make a stand. "You're right. I've found what I was looking for, what was missing from my life, and I'm through running. I'll deal with what comes and make the most of it. I want a life in Dunmuir, and though I'm still not sure what that will entail, I'm going to give it the shot it deserves."

He smiled and her heart beat a little easier. "That's all I'm asking for, love."

"Yeah—asking. I don't exactly recall a whole lot of question marks in that statement of yours." She burst out laughing—and it amazed her that he could still set her at ease, despite everything. "Now are you going to take me to see my father or should I start walking?"

He linked his hand with hers and brought it to his lips. "Let's go, love."

When they got to the hospital and walked into her father's room, it was to find he was awake and being kept company by two men in their twenties, their resemblance to him hard to miss. Reddish hair, blue eyes. They looked just like him—just like her.

She stopped short, her breathing shallow as her pulse raced. These were her brothers, her father. It was everything she'd hoped for, yet she felt like a stranger intruding on a private moment. Worse still, she was the reason Rory had been shot. If he hadn't tried to save her, if she hadn't gone looking for him, he'd never have been injured.

"I'm sorry to interrupt. I can come back." She was already spinning on her heels when Angus put a steadying hand on her shoulder and motioned with a tilt of her head to the people behind her.

She turned back to them and found her brothers standing there by her father's side. There was a long pause of silence between them, and then the eldest of the brothers stepped towards her.

"I'm Niall and this is my younger brother, Finnean. It's a pleasure to meet ye, lass." Niall extended his hand, but when she took it expecting a shake, he pulled her into a hearty embrace. "Ye're family now."

Niall let her go, and Finnean gave her another hug, relief flooding through her, her heart overwhelmed with emotion. "It really is a pleasure."

They both shook Angus's hand, and got the introductions out of the way, before Niall grabbed his brother. "I could do with a coffee. We'll be back in just a few."

Angus quickly kissed the top of her head and joined her brothers, so it was now just her and her father. She sat down in the seat near the bed, quickly taking him in. He looked a bit pale, which made his freckles stand out, but his blue eyes were clear and attentive, kind and intelligent. "How are you feeling?"

"I'll manage, lass." Rory reached out and took her hand, giving it a squeeze. "I can't tell ye how happy ye've made me. Yer mother... she meant the world to me, and I can't apologize enough for not being there for ye. I can only hope ye'll let me be a part of yer life now."

She blinked back tears, so many uncertainties, so many insecurities melting away. "I'd really like that."

Back at the hotel, Rowan sat by Angus's side, waiting for the pregnancy test to develop, each second feeling like a year. Rowan was happier than she had been in the longest of times, yet waiting for the results had her on edge.

She didn't know how to feel about it. Things were finally working out for her, and she now had more than she'd ever hoped for. Once again, she had a family and a place to call home. And she had Angus. She couldn't ask for a truer friend. Yet he was so much more to her. She couldn't imagine a life without him in it.

Angus gave her hand a squeeze. "It's time, love."

He picked it up and held it between them, so they could both look at once. There. Staring up at her was a minus sign, making her heart ache when she should be relieved. "I'm not pregnant. That's a good thing, right?"

"Och, love. I can't really answer that for ye. I know the circumstances wouldn't have been ideal, but I'll admit, I couldn't imagine a more perfect mother or partner." He brushed her cheek, his fingers tangled in her hair. "I love ye, Rowan. With all that I am, I love ye."

She then realized what had been staring her in the face all along. He was her very heart and soul. All that she was, and all she would be, he made better, and her life wouldn't be complete without him in it. She couldn't ask for a better man, a better friend. "Well, I'm glad to hear it, because I think you've managed to charm and finagle your way into my heart. I've fallen madly in love with you, Angus Macleod. There'll be no getting rid of me now."

He threw his head back and laughed before kissing her full on the lips. "I'm glad to hear it, lass. Though old crabbit MacDougal will be sorely disappointed that he's out of the running. Now what do ye say we head home and give the locals something new to gossip about. I'm sure we could think of something shocking and scandalous to get up to if left to our own devices."

She smiled and kissed him, her heart filled to the brim. "I couldn't think of a more perfect way to spend the time."

The End

A Highland Heist, book three in the Contemporary Highland Series, is now available. For updates, please check http://calimackay.com.

www.ingramcontent.com/pod-product-compliance
Lightning Source LLC
Chambersburg PA
CBHW050936120626
46552CB00001B/239